MY FOREVER
Love

JP SAYLE

Warning
Some of the content of this book is sexually graphic, with the use of explicit language and adult situations involving two males. It is only intended for mature audiences.

Books by the author

Ferron's Journey: Revelation Part Three (book six)

Mine, Body and Soul Trilogy

Ferron's Journey Trilogy

The Billionaire Playground Series

Property of a Billionaire (Book one)

The Manx Cat Guardians Series

Where it all Began: Origins (Book 1)

Seeing Beyond the Scars (Book 2)

Destiny Collides Past and Present (Book 3)

Searching for a Soul to Love (Book 4)

The 12 Disasters of Christmas (Book 5)

Laws of Attraction (Book 6)

The Teacher's Boy (Book 7)

Boxset

Audio Books

Mine, Body and Soul, Part One: The Playroom Series

Mine, Body and Soul, Part Two: The Playroom Series

Mine, Body and Soul, Part Three: The Playroom Series

Daddy Kink: The App (book one)

Always More: The Flamingo Bar (book one)

When Fake Changed Everything

Ferron's Journey: Damaged Part One

Ferron's Journey: Hidden Part Two

Story Outline

My Forever Love
(Spin off Story from The Playroom Series)

Can Isaac plan a surprise wedding, despite Ferron deciding to help out a friend and landing them with two babies to help care for?

Isaac had everything under control, or so he thought. His secret plans to wed Ferron on New Year's Day were going without a hitch. Then Ferron offered to let Seth and his twin daughters move in with them just a few weeks before the wedding.
As the girls throw their lives into turmoil and their home upside down, will Isaac be able to keep the wedding a secret and on track?

Only time will tell.

Over the last year Ferron has suffered and it feels only right that he should get his HEA

Prologue

FERRON

The excitement buzzed through me as our taxi got closer to Juyongguan, one of the most popular parts of the Great Wall. Although I'd enjoyed the hustle and bustle of Beijing, it was only as we'd driven out into the countryside that I'd really started to appreciate China's beauty. Juyongguan was a hilly part of the region, the wall climbing up into dense forested mountains. The scent of an overpopulated Beijing was already a memory as fresh air filled the car through an open window.

Isaac had been gutted when our driver had informed us the previous day that mist had covered the top of the wall. Therefore, we'd postponed our trip until today when the weather forecast was better.

The cloudless blue sky that had greeted us as we'd looked outside our hotel window had perked Isaac up that morning. Not that he'd been miserable the day before, not once we'd gone and explored the Xidan area, close to our hotel, instead. We'd walked twenty-five minutes to the Forbidden City before moving on to Tiananmen Square. Isaac had stopped grumping about the weather the moment that we'd reached the Forbidden City.

The trip had revealed the hidden history buff side of Isaac. He was like a nerdy school pupil, spouting reams of information about everything we saw. We hadn't needed a guide because Isaac knew it all. I'd long since given up being shocked at all the information he could reel off if I asked a question. When I'd planned the trip, I'd had no idea how much he'd get from the experience, or how much I would from sharing his joy.

The last three months since the end of the court case had been wonderful, but with one exception—Wren.

I'd learned that I was far from patient, and with every day that passed without Wren coming back safe, a little part of me had died. I'd avoided talking about it to Isaac, knowing that he was already worried enough about it. Isaac had informed me that the security team were still working closely with the police, but he hadn't been able to tell me anything more.

Was Wren alive? A shudder rippled down my spine. *Stop it. Remember that dwelling on this won't make any difference.*

Doing my best to listen to the voice of reason, I pushed the nagging thought to the back of my mind, not wanting to spoil the day. Instead I concentrated on the weeks of planning I'd done after receiving the money from the sale of the house. It had no sooner hit my bank account before I'd headed to the travel agents. Nathan had been cool about only being given four weeks' notice. I'd managed to keep another part of the trip secret though, paying an astronomical price once we'd got to the airport for two first class seats to Beijing. Even though I'd winced when I'd handed over my debit card, it had been well worth it. We'd arrived in Beijing refreshed and ready for the holiday. It was definitely the way to travel.

As the car started to slow, I clutched at my backpack, trying to focus on the gorgeous scenery. But it was like the tiny box hidden in my bag was attempting to burn a hole through the fabric as it touched my leg.

I sucked in a shaky breath, praying that I wasn't about to make a huge fool of myself. *He loves me. He loves me.* I continued to repeat it as I clutched at my backpack with sweaty hands. Needing a distraction, I turned to face Isaac. His face was a picture of awe, all his previous stress gone. His mouth opened, but no words came out as the car drew to halt and we got our first proper look at a part of the Great Wall.

My gaze shifted between the specular wall and Isaac as he went all nerdy on me. "Did you know that the Great Wall of China is basically a series of fortification systems built across the northern borders of China to protect the territories? There's a whole bunch of information about the arseholes who tried to cause upset, but I won't bore you with that. It's reckoned though, that parts of the wall were built as early as the seventh century. The most well-known sections of it were said to be built by the Ming dynasty in the fourteenth century. It seems that old Ming saw the potential of fortifying the wall so that he could control more of the country."

Some of what he'd said was lost in excitement as he exited the car. He stood out in a crowd, his height making him impossible to miss, the huge throng of people parting as he walked towards the tourist access point in order to climb up the tower.

His voice carried as he continued to speak, completely unaware of whether I was behind him or not. I gave our driver, Qin, a wave, chuckling as I raced to catch up with Isaac. Qin, who spoke perfect English, had been provided by the hotel. He'd wait while we explored. Therefore, I didn't pay him any more attention as I caught up with Isaac, who was still talking.

"Apart from defense, other purposes of the Great Wall included border controls and allowing the imposition of duties on goods transported along the Silk Road. It also regulated the control of immigration and emigration. I think they used the towers as a defense as well. There are watchtowers, troop barracks and garrison stations scattered along the length of it." He grinned at me, taking hold of my hand and tugging me along with him. I panted as I tried to keep up.

Isaac stepped past several people, continuing to keep his gaze focused on the wall which stretched for miles. I'd never considered how immense the thing might be, or how tiny I'd feel in comparison as we started to walk up the steep slope which led towards the top of the first tower.

By the time we got to the top I was sweaty and more than a little out of breath. Isaac on the other hand, looked like he'd been sat for an hour having a rest. But his excitement was contagious as I followed his gaze. *Holy fuck!* The view of the wall weaving through the mountains was spectacular. I tightened my grip on Isaac's hand. "It's stunning. Imagine that this has been here for all these years!"

"Today, the Great Wall is generally recognized as one of the most impressive architectural feats in history. It's fucking amazing." He moved his gaze to mine, and there was the love I was used to seeing shining out of his face. "Thank you, little man. This is the best gift that anyone has ever given me."

The utter sincerity in his voice gave me a warm glow, and I contemplated whether coming here was about Isaac's need to visit this magnificent place, or more about my own journey. The wall had stood for many years and had been witness to many battles. Yet, it had survived and strengthened over the years so that it could continue to endure. My heart swelled as I kept my gaze locked with Isaac's. He was my Great Wall. He'd suffer for me, in order to keep me safe, no matter what happened.

I stepped closer to him, releasing his hand so that I could open my bag. I took it as a sign when my fingers found the tiny box I'd been carrying around with me for weeks without having to break eye contact. Pulling it out of the bag, I dropped my backpack on the ground. The thud it made had Isaac glancing down. His mouth opened and closed, though, once his gaze landed on my hand.

Everything around us seemed to disappear as his gaze moved to mine, his eyes shimmering in the light. The warmth of the sun penetrated my T-shirt as I exhaled shakily before getting down on one knee. My ears buzzed and I struggled to swallow as my mouth dried up.

The touch of the ground beneath my knee seemed to centre me as I licked my lips. "I love you. There isn't a day that goes by that I don't pinch myself to remind me of how lucky I am that you feel the same way. The journey we've been on has been a hard one, and although I might have got through it on my own, you made all the difference between existing and living." My fingers trembled as I opened up the small velvet box which housed a platinum band, our initials intertwined around it. I'd known from the first moment that I'd seen the ring that it would be perfect for Isaac.

I held the box out towards Isaac. "Will you marry me?" I held my breath as he stood there, unmoving, for what felt like an eternity. Then he swept me off my feet and I was swung around as he whooped loudly.

"You're making me dizzy," I cried out, trying to hold on to both him and the ring box as he continued to swing me around. When he eventually lowered me to the floor, quite a crowd had gathered, but I ignored them as I waited for him to answer my question.

"Oh, you slay me, little man." He lowered his forehead to mine as he cupped my cheeks, his gaze filled with a happiness that left me breathless and even giddier than I was already. "Yes, I'll marry you. Today, tomorrow, whenever. I don't care as long as you're mine forever."

"I like the sound of that." I took the ring from the box, his hands falling from my face as I stepped back. I took hold of his left hand, and to the sounds of cheers slipped the ring on his finger. I repeated his own words back to him. "Mine, forever."

"Always," he responded in a choked voice.

I bent and picked up my backpack, shoving the box back inside before throwing it over my shoulder. I reached for his hand. "Let's go and explore so that you can carry on showing off your nerdy geek side."

He huffed, but his face was full of amusement as he interlinked his fingers with mine, starting to reel off more information about the wall.

My lips curled into a smile, the ring on his finger glinting in the sunlight as our joined hands swung between us.

Could life get any better than this?

The sun was shining and I was on holiday with the man I loved who'd just agreed to marry me. What more could a guy ask for?

Absolutely nothing.

One

As I stared at the beautiful ring on my hand, which Ferron had given me in China at the Great Wall, my head was full of what I wanted to happen next. To say I'd been stunned by his romantic proposal was the understatement of the century. But there'd been no question in my mind what my answer was going to be. He'd been it for me from the moment I'd laid eyes on him, and though it had taken years for me to get the courage to go after what I'd wanted, I'd grabbed on with both hands when I had.

For several weeks, since we'd got back from China, the past had been on my mind. I'd wasted so much time that Ferron had gone through a journey I wouldn't wish on my worst enemy. With that on constant replay, I'd come to the conclusion that we shouldn't be wasting any more time waiting, and that included getting married. As yet, we'd not talked about the wedding plans, but they were never far from my thoughts.

Was Ferron thinking we needed to leave an allotted period of time before we decided on getting hitched? I eyed the man in question, who was busy collecting empty glasses in the full club.

"You do know that there's been a customer trying to get your attention for the last five minutes, while you've been staring at Ferron, right?" came a voice from the opening at the end of the bar.

I glanced at Sam, who held a file in his hand, which I assumed was why he was down here and not up in the Flamingo bar. He pointed to the sub who was hopping from one foot to another as he eyed me hopefully. I swallowed a sigh and went to take his order, not answering Sam.

By the time I'd filled several orders for soft drinks, as there was no alcohol served on nights when the club was open for people to play freely, Sam had perched himself on a stool. "Aren't you supposed to be working upstairs?"

"Yeah, but I'm sure Scott has everything in hand. You look like you might need someone to talk to?" Sam gave me an encouraging grin and I felt myself weaken.

Signalling to Tyler that I was going to take five, I stepped to the end of the bar and beckoned for Sam to follow me. Tyler, one of the other barmen, was more than capable and he had Eddy to keep up with the steady stream of people wanting a drink.

Before I opened the storeroom door, I checked to make sure that Ferron was busy. I didn't want him to catch me talking to Sam about the idea that was forming in my mind. When the door shut behind Sam, I leant against it, taking no chances of being interrupted.

"You're not planning on murdering me and trying to hide me in here are you?" Sam joked as he eyed the door I was leant against.

"Maybe, if you don't keep up to date with the spreadsheets next time I go on holiday," I fired back.

Sam hunched and a scowl appeared on his face. "Let's not talk about that, or what happened while you were away."

Laughter was right there, waiting to come out at how forlorn he looked with a childish pout on his mouth. I'd heard his two partners, Jake and Bailey, had come to help him. By all accounts it had been an entertaining night for the staff, but not for Sam.

"I can see your lips twitching, man, don't you dare laugh, or I won't help you with whatever your problem is."

I sobered at that and shrugged, trying to act nonchalant, even though it was the last thing I was feeling. I wet my lips. "I want to plan a surprise wedding for Ferron, and I want to get married on New Year's Day. I think Nathan will let me use the Flamingo Bar as they aren't planning to open, so it's free. I'm sure I can talk Lenny and Carl into catering for it." As I continued to lay out my thoughts as they came to me, Sam stood frozen to the spot.

His mouth opened, but no words came out as his eyes grew to the size of saucers. "You're kidding, right?"

His voice was a strangled whisper and my gut clenched. "You think it's a bad idea?"

"Fuck no. I think it's perfect and so romantic, especially after how Ferron started last New Year."

Ferron had spent the previous year unconscious in hospital, attached to a ventilator. He'd been kidnapped by a scary fucker who liked to torture subs for pleasure. "Yeah, that's what I thought. Leave the past behind and start the New Year with something amazing."

Sam rubbed his hands together as his eyes got a gleam in them, which didn't help my knotted stomach. "Right, I think we should get as many people to help as possible so that it's not obvious to Ferron something is up. We can allocate tasks to everyone. Oh, I'll have to come up with a plan for his stag party—"

"What? No, that will give the game away for sure!"

It appeared Sam didn't hear me as he continued excitedly. "I'll leave you to sort yours with Nathan and get Lenny and maybe Adam to help with Ferron's. From what I heard, Lenny did a great job with Adam's stag earlier this year."

Recalling how worried I'd been when I'd got home to find Ferron gone the night Lenny had invited him to Adam's stag party, I clamped my lips together to stop myself from saying something that might upset Sam when it was obvious he was excited about helping me.

His lips pursed and he wore a thoughtful expression. "Yes, I think we can do this." He met my worried gaze. "I'll look up some websites that organise weddings and see what they suggest we need to do. What about budget?"

A strangled moan rose as I shook my head. "I've got money, just don't go wild. I don't want to go bankrupt over this."

"Cool, I'm good at budgeting...with my own money," he quickly added on when my brow arched, causing his face to flush bright red.

"Well as long as you're good with secrets, we'll be okay. We've eight weeks, do you think we can pull it off?"

"Erm, of course. It'll all be fine, you mark my words."

I loved his confidence, but the itch at the base of my neck wasn't quite convinced.

22

Two

What was wrong with Isaac? He was like a cat on a hot tin roof, only he wasn't giving his feet a chance to settle at all. The man in question was currently pacing in front of the large window that overlooked the Downs. Usually when he went to the window, he'd stand and stare out, but his current behaviour was at complete odds with that.

"Are you going to come sit and watch the film with me?"

He spun to face me and the smile he gave me was apologetic. "Yes. Sorry, I've a...few things...going on...at work," he finished in a rush as he looked anywhere but at me.

Is he lying to me?

I tilted my head and chewed my lower lip between my teeth, all the while keeping my gaze on him. He shifted uncomfortably before he made a move to come and sit next to me.

"Have I done something to upset you?" I'd got much braver over the last few months about voicing questions, even when I felt like I wanted to puke, like right now.

Immediately he lifted me until I was sat in his lap, a place I loved to be. I placed my hand over his heart and felt his erratic heartbeat.

"You've done absolutely nothing wrong, little man. I'm being weird, aren't I?" he said, with a resignation that set my limbs to quiver.

"Yes, and it's making me freak out a little. You've been weird ever since last week when you took Sam into the storeroom for a chat." I'd not missed how they'd disappeared, or how Sam had been all beaming smiles whereas Isaac looked like he'd swallowed something distasteful.

He sighed and stroked a hand down the side of my face. "You saw that, did you?"

I waited a beat for him to explain, but when he wasn't forthcoming, I swallowed hard. "Why did you look upset after he left?"

"I wasn't upset, more...anxious." His eyes shut for a moment, and my heart stuttered in my chest before they re-opened and I saw a fierce light of determination. "I'm planning a surprise for you—"

"Oh, a surprise, I love surprises! Oh what is it?" I squealed in delight as I squirmed on Isaac's lap. I didn't fail to miss how his body reacted to me, but I ignored it for the moment, quickly thinking about ways to get him to tell me what the surprise was.

"That look on your face, you can forget it. I'm not spilling the beans. You'll have to wait to see what it is."

I did a little more squirming as I stroked the thin T-shirt covering his hairy chest. I lowered my eyelashes and gave him a sexy smile, confident that I could break him. "You know I'm terrible at waiting." To prove a point, I did a little hip wiggle, making sure to grind down on the plumping cock beneath me.

He groaned long and low as the hand on my cheek moved to slide down my neck and a second later, he was kissing me gently. Isaac took his time, deepening the kiss only when I opened for him. His lips were full and firm, and tasted sweet.

My groan of approval matched his as his hand disappeared up the back of my jumper and he caressed my naked back. His fingertips traced patterns on my skin as he sucked on my tongue when I pushed it into his mouth.

"Such a beautiful boy," he gasped as his mouth trailed down the side of my neck. His beard rubbed against my skin, creating a tingling warmth. "Do you think the movie could wait till later?"

His other hand was already untying the strings on my loose jog pants.

Nodding, I panted as his fingers took hold of my hard cock and stroked me from base to tip. His hand did a little twisty thing at the mushroom head, gathering my pre-cum to use as lube. I cried out as his hand slid down my hard length. Lost in the moment, all thoughts of what the surprise was seemed unimportant as he brought me pleasure.

His mouth and tongue worked to undermine my control as the pace of his strokes increased. Each and every time he reached the head of my cock, he collected my pre-cum. His hand was slick and perfect on my skin.

I clenched my arse cheeks as I ground down against his lap, and he mewled, but his lips didn't stop what they were doing to my neck. I had a moment to wonder if I'd end up with a hickey before the hand stroking my back disappeared and Isaac maneuvered me so I was straddling his lap, facing him.

"Kiss me," he growled, his expression strained with controlled desire.

His heavy-lidded onyx eyes held me entranced as I shifted and licked at the seam of his lips. "Open for me, Daddy," I whispered seductively. Something else he'd given me was the confidence to ask for what I wanted, safe in the knowledge he wanted to give me everything my heart desired.

When he did as I asked without hesitation, my heart thrummed with heady excitement. "Such a good Daddy," I whispered against his parted lips before I claimed his mouth in a hot, wet kiss.

The hand in my pants went back to stroking me as I rocked my hips, using my arse to bring pleasure to Isaac. His chest heaved as sweat gathered around my hairline, and I placed my hands on his huge shoulders, increasing my pace while not releasing his mouth.

Heat from the burning fire behind me added to the warmth flowing through me, but I didn't want to stop to take off my clothes, not when I was so close to coming. My balls were throbbing and my tailbone was tingling like mad.

There was a long second where I hung right on the edge, suspended in the intense feelings coursing through me, then Isaac took control back from me and I was lost. The moment he sucked hard on my tongue and squeezed the head of my cock, cum spurted onto his hand.

I cried out into his mouth while he continued to milk me dry. His large body stiffened beneath me and I thrust down a little harder.

"Fuck yeah, little man, fuck, I love you," he cried out in a strangled voice as he released my mouth, his head falling back against the cushion of the sofa as if he couldn't hold it up. His large body rippled with shudders as his cock bucked against my backside.

I flopped against his chest and laid my head on his shoulder, gasping. His chest heaved in time with mine for several minutes as we lay in a comfortable silence.

"I think the film will have to wait a bit longer, I'm a sticky mess," Isaac mumbled against the top of my head before he kissed my hair.

I shifted back and grinned happily, "A naked, wet Daddy? I can totally get behind that."

Isaac groaned. "I've created a monster."

When he didn't sound in the least bit bothered, I shrugged. "You have and you love it."

"That I do," he answered as he shifted forward. Still holding me, he stood, the show of power making my cock twitch. "But you have to give this old man a chance to recover if you want round two."

I giggled as he walked towards the hallway. "I'll give you as long as it takes to get clean, so I can make you dirty again."

He heaved a sigh that I was sure he thought was supposed to sound put upon, but didn't in the slightest, as we crested the top of the stairs.

"Can you die from too much sex?"

This time I let out a full on belly laugh. "Just think, it'll be a great way to go," I said through the laughter.

"Keep laughing and someone might find themselves with a punishment."

The threat was totally empty, given his punishments to me were usually lovely rewards. It brought back what we'd been talking about before he'd distracted me. "Now, what was this about a surprise?"

Three

Two weeks and still Ferron hadn't let up about the surprise. I had to give it to him, he was a tenacious little bugger, and he was driving me nuts! Since the day I'd mentioned it, he'd been coming up with increasingly ingenious ways to try and get me to talk.

The latest one was a sudden obsession with sexy underwear, which he'd slip into right before we went to work. It drove me nuts because he never wore it when we were home alone. No, the little shit was teasing me, and I have to say, I was on the brink of confessing all just to see him in bed with his lacy boy shorts.

As the image wormed its way past my defences, my cock started to stiffen, and I cursed.

"What's up with you?" Nathan growled as he glanced from me to the stack of invoices that I was using as a pretence to come up to the Flamingo Bar to talk about the wedding.

"Ferron is what's up!" I exclaimed, then, at the alarmed look on Nathan's face as his head shot up, I quickly explained. "He's driving me to distraction because I stupidly told him I was planning a surprise for him."

"Why did you do that for pity's sake?"

I shrugged and scratched at my head. "He caught me off guard, and he has this sad look he gets and, well—"

"You're a sucker," Nathan stated, his face full of humour.

"And you're not?" I fired back, causing his amusement to disappear and be replaced by a scowl. Lenny, Nathan's boyfriend, had him wrapped around his little finger.

"Point taken, but I'm not the one keeping secrets, am I? Anyway, talking of secrets, I've managed to source all the things you asked me for to decorate the room. Boyd is going to build you an arch with two large playing cards on either side. He's also got a couple of his carpenters to create a massive teapot, cup, and saucer. The company I got the stuffed flamingos from has a very large caterpillar and giant rabbit. They look really cool and should be here next week.

"I have to say, when you said you wanted to go with a Mad Hatter's winter-themed wedding, I was a little sceptical, but you know, I think it works. Have you seen the cake that Lenny has designed for you, yet?" Nathan glanced at the entrance to the kitchen where Carl and Lenny were working today. When I shook my head, Nathan lowered his voice. "Whatever you do, don't mention the cake to Carl. He's miffed that I asked Lenny."

I chuckled at Nathan's expression as he gave another furtive glance at the closed kitchen door like Carl was about to burst through it. Once he was back to looking at me he continued in a whisper, "Lenny's cakes taste far superior to Carl's, and if you tell him I said that, I'll sack you."

With a struggle, I kept myself from laughing aloud. "Right, boss."

"Oh, shut up, I'm the one helping you sort out your secret wedding," Nathan declared loudly.

It was my turn to check that no one was within earshot. "Keep it down will you," I hissed, thankful that neither Benny nor Shaun were paying us any attention as they set up the bar, ready for opening.

Nathan's face smoothed out as he gave me an apologetic smile. "So, what's left to tick off the list of jobs that need doing for," he leant closer to me and whispered, "the secret wedding?"

I rolled my eyes heavenward. *Please give me patience.*

"Oh, and what are we doing about a stag party? Lenny has come up with an idea to invite Ferron and the boys up to the apartment, selling it as a kind of sub pre-Christmas party thing," Nathan added before I could say anything.

"He's already mentioned it to Ferron as he's asked to swap a shift with Seth, not that I'm counting on Seth turning up," I said. "There is something going on, and he's getting really flaky with his attendance at work. I've already spoken to him twice. I've told him a third time and he's out."

Nathan placed his elbow on the bar and braced as he looked at me with concern. "I didn't realise it had gotten so bad. Why didn't you say something earlier?"

I shifted on my bar stool and eyed the top of the bar, a slither of guilt worming its way to the surface. "I wanted to give him a chance. When his head is in the game, he's great. He works hard, and I know he's been suffering since Rupert dumped him. But lately he looks tired, as if he's not slept. He isn't talking about what's up, and he's started to piss off some of the other guys that he was friendly with. I'm coming up empty as to what is going on with him."

"Maybe I should have a word with him? It was me who took him on," Nathan offered, but he sounded anything but pleased about it.

"Nah, don't worry. I'll have another talk with him, and if that fails, I'll get Ferron to have a go. He's good at getting people to talk."

Nathan snorted. "Yes, you need to remember that, given how hard everyone else is working on keeping your secret. I meant to ask, do you need me to give out any invites? I know neither you nor Ferron have family..." Nathan trailed off, his face losing a little of its colour.

I got a feeling Nathan was wondering if I was going to ask him to be my best man. I was tempted to tease him, knowing how much he didn't enjoy the experience of being Carl's best man. "Stop stressing, I've asked Nix to be my best man."

He sagged, with a look of relief on his face. "Thank God."

"It's a good job I don't easily take offence."

He slapped at my arm, nearly knocking me off my seat. "Watch it," I complained, as I had to hold onto the edge of the bar to stop myself from tipping sideways. I wasn't a lightweight by any stretch of the imagination, but Nathan had the biggest biceps I'd ever seen.

"Sorry, I forget that you're not as strong as me."

"Fuck off. Shall we get back to what we were talking about before I have to go back downstairs to work?" I asked, raising my brows.

Four

I watched Seth as he rubbed at his heavy-lidded eyes. The dark circles and empty expression worried me because I remembered how I'd looked when I'd been held captive by...Devon. A shiver ran down my spine before I could shove the thought away and get Devon out of my head.

Seth clearly wasn't being held captive, but he looked like he was being tortured by something. His mouth was set in a grim line as he moved to the bar to serve the customer who'd just walked up. He didn't offer a friendly smile like he used to. It seemed to take all his effort to ask the guy on the other side of the bar what he wanted.

I twisted around to search for Isaac and sighed in relief when he was busy at the other end of the bar, talking to Adam and Carl. Isaac had mentioned his concern for Seth to me, so I took the opportunity to try and see if I could find out what was wrong. I waited until Seth had finished serving before going to him. "Seth, can you help me in the glass room for a minute?"

His gaze swept the bar before it came back to me and he nodded. I steeled my spine, and the second the door closed on the busy bar, I pounced. "What's wrong?"

He blinked in the way a person who's not had time to wake up tends to do. "I'm not sure what you mean." His answer was delivered in a flat tone.

The lack of emotion was scary when he was one of the few subs who knew my background. "You know about my past, Seth...is someone hurting you?" I was beyond pleased I'd managed to get the words out, even if my voice was full of nerves.

"I...what?" He blanched. "No, no, definitely not."

"If it's not that, then what is it? I'm worried about you. You look dreadful..." the words dried on my lips as big, fat tears rolled down his face.

"Please don't say anything. I'm struggling with my baby girls and I don't know what to do." He hiccupped and sobbed as he wiped at the tears continuing to run down his pale cheeks.

My eyes widened at this information. Had Isaac mentioned that Seth had children? A flutter of jealousy at him being a father was instantly quashed by his anguished expression.

Children were a secret dream I'd hidden from Isaac. With everything that had happened to me, and the ongoing investigation into the Dom's Haven, there was no way I'd mention it to him. He didn't need the added pressure of giving me something I wanted when he had enough on his plate.

I shook off the feeling of regret. "Isaac never mentioned you had children."

"He doesn't know, no one does. Please, don't tell anyone, they'll take my twin girls away from me."

The panic was gut-wrenching, and I couldn't stop myself from wrapping an arm around his shaking shoulders. "Why will they take the girls off you?"

His body shuddered against mine. "Rupert constantly said I wasn't fit to look after the girls." His bitterness reminded me of how I felt about Devon's constant belittling of me. "That didn't stop him from leaving me and our babies though."

He looked at me with tear-drenched eyes as my heart ached for him. "I'm trying to keep everything together. Rupert signed the house over to me, so the girls have a roof over their heads, but that was all he did. Well, besides signing full custody of the girls to me. He wants nothing to do with them. He said that because it was my sperm, they weren't really his, so he's wiped his hands of us. I need this job to pay the bills, but…" he trailed off, then buried his face in my neck and wept.

What a fucking shitty thing to do!

I barely kept the thought to myself as I held on to him, making shushing noises like Isaac did to me when I was upset. By the time he finally lifted his face, it was blotchy, and his eyes were red and swollen.

"Do you feel better for letting it all out?" I knew it was a daft thing to ask, but I always felt a bit better after letting go.

"Actually, I do. I've been holding it together for months. My sister has been helping me out, but she's moving up north to be with her boyfriend, and I don't know what I'm going to do. I've hardly slept for worrying, and when I do, the girls wake needing something from me."

Before I could think about it, words were flowing out of my mouth. "We have a couple of spare rooms; you could move in with us, and we could help out until you figure things out."

The hope that immediately flared to life in his eyes ensured I didn't take back the words, not that I wanted to when I felt excitement starting to bubble through me too. *Isaac isn't going to be happy about this!*

Oh, shut up.

"Do you mean it?" he asked hesitantly.

"Yes, yes, I do. We can help you. I'm sure some of the guys…" I clicked my fingers, recalling how much Eddy had talked about how he'd always wanted children, but his ex-Dom had refused to talk about it. "Eddy, he loves children, and I'm sure he'd help out too. We could set up a rota system to allow you to keep working to pay your bills." I continued to talk, forming a plan of attack as the idea took root.

When I'd finished outlining what I thought would work, Seth looked a little shell-shocked.

"What about Isaac, do you think he'll agree?"

As if the man in question had heard his name, the door opened, and his head appeared around it. Seth baulked, and I felt a flush of heat creep up my neck as Isaac looked between us before he stepped fully into the room.

Oh shit, how was I going to tell him what I'd done?

The hope to catch him alone to talk about this after I'd come up with a way to approach the subject, disappeared with his inquisitive stare.

I exhaled shakily.

Don't let him say no!

My eyes teared up at the thought, but seeing the instant concern on his face, I tried to blink them back. As I walked to him, one lone tear fell down my cheek. "Seth's in serious trouble and needs our help."

Instantly Isaac put his beefy arm around me and looked at Seth, who'd made a choking kind of sound. I didn't dare look at him for fear Isaac would know I was about to ask for something huge.

"What's going on, Seth?" The apprehension in his voice matched his expression.

Seth gave a quick run through of what he'd said to me and Isaac got a look of distress on his face.

"Do you think we could help out? You know, let Seth and the girls move into the spare rooms until he finds someone to help him after his sister goes?" Deep lines marred Isaac's brow, so I begged shamelessly. "Please, Isaac, we can ask some of the other guys if they want to help out too." I gave him my best sorrowful look as he groaned.

His lips puffed out as he blew out a breath, a look of resignation appearing on his face before he slowly nodded at me. "Okay, little man, but just until Seth gets himself sorted."

"Oh, thank you, you don't know what a life-saver you are," Seth cried as he came to us, wrapping his arms around us both as best he could.

Isaac mumbled something under his breath that I didn't quite catch, but the resignation remained when Seth released us. Making a silent promise to make it up to him later, I offered up my lips for a kiss. When he obliged me, my stomach settled.

The moment Isaac's mouth released mine, I glanced at Seth. "When is your sister leaving?"

"She's moving out in a fortnight. She wants to be with her boyfriend for Christmas. That's okay, right?"

Isaac stilled against me, but I was too excited at the prospect of having babies in the house for Christmas to pay any real attention to him. "That's great, isn't it, Isaac? I love Christmas."

"Yeah, great," he responded without any real enthusiasm, but again I ignored it, thinking how the babies would take away any doubts he had.

Five

ISAAC

"What are you playing at?" Lenny demanded, the second I opened my front door to him. In his hands was a large cake box, and I got a sinking feeling I'd missed something when I met the one blue eye not covered by the red hair that had fallen over the side of his face.

"Okay, you might want to fill me in."

He grunted and sidestepped me, heading into the house. I shut out the chilly December air and followed him down the hall into the lounge room at a slower pace, trying to recall what had been in my calendar.

The thing was, I was too tired to recall my own name, what with all the running around I'd been doing trying to get ready for a wedding that was just two weeks away. Then there were the girls, Cheryl and Julie. Jesus, they were the most adorable girls, and my heart skipped several beats as I tried to quell the emotions that came at the thought of how stunned I'd been by seeing Ferron holding the thirteen-month-old Julie in his arms.

Right at that moment, I'd let go of my frustration at being caught with my pants down, when Ferron had shanghaied me into letting Seth and his girls move in with us. It hadn't taken long to figure out that Ferron had used his tears against me. I'd been unsure if I should be angry or impressed that he had it in him to manipulate me. How could I be cross with him or Seth when they'd both looked so happy?

I shook my head, recalling how much fun, and money, Ferron had spent getting the spare room ready for the girls. Did Ferron want children of his own?

The question was one I'd asked myself quite a lot over the last week, with the amount of time Ferron spent with the girls. They had turned into the greatest distraction for Ferron, and he'd stopped asking about my secret. Only thing was, they distracted me too.

Resignedly, I met Lenny's heated stare as I walked to the sofa and sat while he made himself at home, warming himself in front of the roaring fire. "What didn't I do?"

He pointed to the large box he'd placed on the coffee table. "What day is it today?" His foot tapped soundlessly on the carpeted floor as I frowned at him, unable to come up with an answer. "Cake fucking tasting day!" he growled loudly.

About to tell him to keep his voice down, the monitor on the sofa squawked to life and there was a cry. I was up off the sofa and heading for the door in a heartbeat. I paused in the doorway and glanced back at Lenny, knowing if one of the girls was awake from their nap the other would be in a matter of minutes. "Come on, you can get one of the girls."

"What, me? Oh no, I told you before, I don't do babies," he squealed, sounding rather a lot like a baby himself.

The cries coming from the monitor increased, and as predicted, there was a second set of lungs joining the first. Panic at their distress rode up fast, as it did every time the two little mites cried. "Stop that nonsense and get your arse moving, they need us."

I didn't wait to see if he'd follow as I took the stairs two at a time, puffing slightly as I opened the door to their bedroom. The second they saw me, they both stopped crying and lifted their arms. Having never thought of myself as paternal, the smile that spread over my face, while my heart clenched in my chest, once again surprised me. "There's my girls. What's all this fuss about, hey?"

My nose twitched as I got closer to the two cots that sat side by side, my stomach dropping as I heaved and struggled not to suck in another stinky breath. How the fuck could two little people make such a smell? I cursed that I'd not come up with an excuse to not have the girls this morning while Seth had gone to sort out his home and grab more of their stuff to bring back here.

"Jeez, what is that smell?" Lenny asked from behind me.

"A dirty nappy," I muttered, still trying to hold my breath and figure out which one the smell was coming off. I had every intention of passing that twin to Lenny, knowing my stomach would rebel if I had to change the stinky bum. I refused to think how much Ferron had laughed at my ham-handed efforts with a dirty nappy.

Figuring it was Julie, who seemed to poo for Britain, I reached for Cheryl, only to sigh as I cupped her tiny bottom and felt the squishy nappy. Her warm, tiny body wriggled in my arms, making the stench increase.

Her small hands went straight for my beard and she ran her little fingers through it, making a cooing noise that I was a total sucker for. The scent, though breath-taking, was momentarily forgotten as she looked into my eyes and gave me the biggest grin, revealing her four tiny teeth. Drool ran out of her mouth as she started to talk in baby gibberish.

"Is that right, baby girl? Tell Isaac all about it," I replied in a childish voice.

"Get you, man. Where's my phone? I need to record this because Nathan is never gonna believe me that you're talking like a little girl."

"Fu...shut up and grab Julie, she'll kick off in a minute if you don't get her out of the cot," I warned, knowing that she had more of a temper and liked to express herself—loudly.

"Geez, I wish I'd just rung you. Why did I think I'd be doing you a favour by bringing the cake here?" Lenny continued to complain as he reached into the cot and Julie made a kind of squealing sound. "Why is she making that noise?" Lenny questioned in alarm, his arms hanging suspended over the cot, not quite touching Julie who was looking at me with big, sad green eyes.

"She want's Uncle Isaac, don't you, baby girl? I'll give you a cuddle downstairs once I've changed Cheryl."

Her lower lip trembled, and a golf ball seemed to lodge itself in my throat.

Lenny stood up and inched back. "Can't you pick them both up? I don't think Julie likes me."

"She hasn't met you is all. Just give her a smile, talk to her, and she'll be fine." I didn't add on the 'I hope'. Julie could be a little temperamental.

The air in my chest rushed out when Julie let Lenny lift her out of the cot without complaint.

Back downstairs, I went to the large window overlooking the Downs where Seth had placed the changing mat, nappies, and wet wipes, hoping the view out the window would distract the girls long enough to let any one of us change their bums.

I eyed the little wriggling girl in my arms and sent up a silent prayer she'd behave. My stomach danced to a frantic tune as I got down on my knees and laid Cheryl on the large mat. She gave me a grin that lulled me into a false sense of security, which lasted all of the thirty seconds it took to take off her little leggings, unclip her vest, and release the Velcro on the reusable nappy.

Breathing through my mouth, I stupidly closed my eyes for a second, bracing for what I was going to find in the nappy. That was when she started to wriggle.

"Holy mother..." I cried, my eyes widened as she attempted to roll over and get up. The nappy moved and the mat beneath became smeared with yellowish poo. It spread up her back as I attempted to grab hold of her legs, the whole while working on not breathing or retching as my stomach started to roil with nausea.

"Oh my god, look at that mess," Lenny pointed out none too helpfully as he stood off to my side, watching me attempt to wrangle with a thirteen-month-old child who was starting to think it was all a big game.

"Help me for pity's sake," I gritted out, trying to keep the smile on my face so I didn't frighten Cheryl, who was giggling and wriggling harder.

"Sorry, man, she's all yours." Just as he spoke, there was a loud farting noise from somewhere in the region of his arms, and a toxic smell quickly followed.

Laughter escaped me, making it hard to hold Cheryl and stop her from creating even more of a mess. "Looks like you're in the same situation. Good luck with that," I said through my laughter as I glanced at Lenny, whose face had bleached of all colour. He eyed the now stinky Julie who was grinning at him like an evil little demon, as if she were a ticking time bomb.

My laughter increased, and Cheryl took the opportunity to kick out and I lost my grip on her. She rolled so fast, all I could do was watch in horror as she got up on her chubby little legs, the nappy dangling down. In slow motion, it appeared to be suspended for a long second before it plopped to the floor as she took off like Usain Bolt, covered in poo.

I scrambled to reach for her, but she was fast and slippy. My hand now covered in toxic poo, I retched, making a gagging noise as Cheryl headed straight for the sofa. My heart dropped as Lenny stood frozen. My dirty hand forgotten, I jumped up a second too late as Cheryl launched herself at the sofa cushions. "No, Cheryl," I shouted.

The sound of a door opening was accompanied by Cheryl making nonsensical baby words, which I was sure were telling me where to get off. Then Seth walked into the room, his gaze sweeping us all before landing on Cheryl.

"What...happened?" His lips quivered, and for a second, I thought he was about to cry, until I saw the mirth in his eyes. He looked between me and Cheryl, who stood leaning against the sofa, a look of cherubic innocence on her tiny face. The edge of the sofa was now coated in slimy yellow poo, much like my hand.

The near paralysing silence that filled the room lasted for no more than two seconds before Lenny could contain himself no more. "Poo-gate, that's what happened," he shouted before he started to belly laugh, clutching at Julie who appeared to find his laughter funny and started to giggle joyfully herself.

When had this become my life?

Six

I eyed Isaac, then the sofa, and tried to keep the smile from appearing. Lenny had rung me, to warn me that Isaac might not be in the best of moods when I got home. "Did you have a good day?" I asked, tongue in cheek, as I sat down on the now clean sofa.

"Lenny told you what happened, didn't he?" Isaac sounded resigned rather than upset, so I nodded. "I told him to keep his mouth shut."

"Come on, it was too funny not to share. At least Seth came back and helped out—"

"What you mean is that he came back to laugh at me. Then he let me retch while I cleaned up Cheryl and he cleaned the sofa."

"I'm sorry." Any hope I had that my apology would improve his long face died when he didn't even glance at me. I crawled into his lap and laid my head on his shoulder, placing a hand on his solid chest. "Do you want me to ask them to move out?" It was the last thing I wanted with Christmas only three days away, and I'd come to love spending time with the two little bundles of joy.

But Isaac was more important to me than anything.

He fidgeted on the seat as the silence lengthened. As I couldn't see his face, I wasn't sure what his issue was, but my insides started to quiver.

"I don't want that." His hand stroked down my back as he spoke. "I...like having the girls here." I'd not missed how many times he'd pick one of the girls up to cuddle them, yet there was something in his voice I couldn't interpret.

I sat up a little so I could see him, then stilled as he asked, "Do you want children?" His voice sounded way too loud in the quiet of the room. I took a few moments to think about how to answer. His face was masked, and I couldn't tell if he'd be pleased or pissed if I answered truthfully.

Remember the chart, tell the truth!

"I do."

His nostrils flared and his eyes darkened, while slashes of deep red flared in his cheeks. "Oh, little man," he muttered before his lips claimed mine in a deep, soul-searing kiss.

It went on and on, until we were both panting and I wanted more than just kisses. All thoughts about babies flew right out the window. "Where's Seth?" I gasped out on a breathy moan.

"He's gone to bed early to try and grab some shuteye as the girls are teething," Isaac replied, while his mouth moved over my jaw. He nibbled his way down my neck, his beard tickling my skin.

Sex had been a little tricky since Seth and the girls had moved in. It tended to happen in the morning during our shower, as it was the furthest point away from the girls and Seth. "Should I go and shut the lounge door and grab the lube?" Isaac had stopped wearing condoms a few months back, after I'd proposed. My arse clenched in anticipation of what was to come.

At his excited nod, I was about to slide off his lap when there was a cry from above. He sighed, and I struggled to keep my lips from forming into a smile at how disgruntled it sounded.

"We could be quiet?" I offered, causing a light to form in Isaac's eyes. It was extinguished a moment later when the first cry was followed by a second, alerting us to the fact that both the girls were now awake.

He nudged me off his lap and towards the door. "Go on, I know you want to go up and see them."

I gave his face a searching stare, and seeing nothing but acceptance, I grinned, then ran to the door, my desire forgotten in my excitement to get cuddles from one of the girls. The smile spread when I heard Isaac follow me. He was just as much of a sucker as I was, no matter how much he tried to hide it.

Two hours later we both crawled exhausted into bed after both girls had taken an age to settle. They'd been tearful and dribbling like a broken tap. Isaac wrapped his arms around me, and I rested my head on his broad shoulder, snuggling into him.

His scent was mixed with that of baby powder and my heart clenched as I recalled that he'd said nothing about my earlier confession. Did he not want a family? We'd never had that type of conversation, so I had no clue as to what he wanted.

Although I was tired, my mind wouldn't rest. My fingers threaded through Isaac's silky chest hair as I traced patterns, then a thought popped into my head. "Why was Lenny here today? He never mentioned why when he talked about poogate."

Isaac, who had been fully relaxed, stiffened against me. "He...erm...yes...he...fuck's sake!" he stuttered and cursed, right before the light came on.

I blinked at the white spots that appeared in front of my eyes. As my vision cleared, Isaac rolled to face me, half his face in shadow because his back was to the small lamp, making it hard to read the emotions running amok over his face.

A shiver of fear ran down my spine. "Is something wrong? Are you...sick?" I whimpered as I voiced my biggest fear. Lenny had been through all manner of surgeries because he'd had issues with his bowel, caused by childhood neglect. He'd ended up with an ileostomy that he'd successfully had reversed last year. Had he come to talk to Isaac because he needed surgery?

His hand stroked down the side of my body before he pulled me closer to him. "Shit! I'm not sick." He moved to rest his forehead against mine, his gaze holding mine as he looked to come to some sort of decision. "I've been planning our secret wedding."

"You what?" I squealed in a shocked voice.

"Shush, you'll wake the girls," he hissed as he tilted his head to listen out for any noise. When there was none, he gave me a sheepish smile, his warm finger pressing against my lips. "I wanted desperately to keep this a secret and surprise you, but with everything that's happened with the girls and Seth moving in, I'm bound to slip up. Lenny came by today because I forgot I was supposed to be doing a cake tasting thing with him. It slipped my mind when Seth asked me to have the girls."

I felt more than saw his shoulders shrug as the sheepish smile remained on his face. I removed his finger from my lips and licked at them. "When are we getting married?" I choked out past my welling emotions. This was really happening, my fiancé was planning *our wedding*.

"New Year's Day." His finger came back to my mouth as it opened, right as my eyes narrowed on him. "Don't shout."

About to disagree, I clamped my lips together. He was right, I would have shouted. *How could I not? I was getting married in ten days' time!* "Seriously?"

He nodded, looking anything but certain.

I sucked in a shaky breath and pushed away the panic. "How on earth can we be ready for a wedding in ten days?" I whispered anxiously. My mind was already racing with all the things you might need to do to make a wedding happen. "I don't even have an outfit! How can I possibly get married?"

He tugged my lip from between my teeth and gave me the sweetest smile. "Tell me this, do you want to get married in ten days?"

"Of course I do. Do I look like a fool to you? But—"

"Then leave all the worrying up to me. I've got everything in hand."

The following evening, as I entered Lenny and Nathan's apartment and saw the layout of the room and all the men gathered for what was supposed to be a little get together for the subs, I realised I'd been hoodwinked.

"This is my stag party, isn't it?" I demanded, pointing at Lenny. His face flushed a bright pink as he glanced about at the other men, who all started to laugh.

"He told you, didn't he?" Lenny didn't need to qualify who 'he' was. I nodded and gave him a beaming smile.

Adam, who had clearly come dressed for a party, sauntered up to Lenny. His dark hair was styled, and he wore slim-fitting black trousers with a gorgeous striped polo top. "It was only a matter of time before he twigged on. How hard has it been to keep it all on the downlow?" he said, slinging his arm over Lenny's shoulders.

Lenny hunched and gave Adam a hard stare. "All you had to do was sort out the wine and listen to Carl whine because he isn't making the cake." He paused as Adam arched his brow. "Okay, you win. Carl whining for weeks must be hell."

"Hey, what about me?" Bailey called from the other side of the large breakfast bar, where there were bottles lined up for cocktail making. "Sam has been so busy with Boyd on making sure the bar looks just right, I've hardly seen him."

"Luke's none too happy with me either because I've been with Sam," Scott piped up from his place on the sofa next to Theo.

Richie, who was sat on the other side of Scott, rubbed his arm. "Just think about how you all get to help Ferron celebrate bringing in a New Year with a huge difference."

A sob caught in the back of my throat at the sentiment as everyone in the room stopped and gave me weepy smiles. "Please, is this supposed to be a stag party or a cry fest?"

"A stag party," Adam stated, his eyes narrowing on me, "but remember, you aren't supposed to ride the flamingos while drinking from a chocolate fountain."

There was a beat before everyone burst out laughing.

Sawyer appeared from down the hallway that led to the bedrooms, then stopped and eyed everyone, his brow wrinkling. "What did I miss?" he asked, sounding put out.

Adam glanced at him. "Oh, don't worry, you've missed nothing. Ferron hasn't gotten to the games part of the evening's entertainment...*yet*."

Seven

C lock watching, it was hard to keep my mind on work. Ferron had gone to Lenny's for his surprise stag party and the plan was that I'd go up and collect him after I'd shut down the club.

My stag party was planned for the following night, not that I was worried about it. I'd made sure to point out to Nix that I had to keep some level of sense with the girls in the house. Seth was going to manage the bar while Ferron and Eddy cared for the twins while I was out.

As predicted by Ferron, Eddy had been more than happy to help. The man seemed to come alive when he was with the girls. His normally quiet demeanour disappeared as he played with them.

I pinched the bridge of my nose and hoped that after tonight's shenanigans, Ferron would be up to the challenge of helping Eddy tomorrow. Ferron wasn't a big drinker, and Adam's cocktails could be lethal.

Eddy nudged my elbow. "I think Nathan is trying to get your attention?"

I glanced towards the end of the bar, where Nathan stood watching me with an unfathomable expression on his face, then back at Eddy. "Thanks."

Strolling towards Nathan, my senses kicked in and my neck itched. "What's up, boss?"

Nathan glanced about before he leaned a little closer to the bar. "Gabriel paid me a visit. It seems that things are about to kick-off at the Dom's Haven. Do you think...do you think it's wise to get married when this shit could turn nasty?" His face turned grim and I cursed silently.

There was a part of me that agreed with Nathan, that wanted to hide Ferron away and not let what was possibly going to happen touch us. But it already had, and with Ferron's excitement still fresh in my mind, I shook my head. "I'm not cancelling the wedding. Devon and his fucking cronies have stolen enough from Ferron. If you'd seen his face this morning, you'd never even make the suggestion to delay. I want him to start this New Year with something positive, goddammit!" I growled angrily.

Nathan placed a hand on my trembling arm as he gave me a fatalistic look. "I get it...I'm just worried."

Convinced he was probably recalling the beating Lenny had been subjected to when Devon had kidnapped the two boys last New Year's Eve, I got why he was worried. Devon was tucked safely behind bars and would be for the next few years, but those at the Dom's Haven were still free to do as they pleased.

There was a clench in my belly as my own fears resurfaced about what could happen to Ferron. I worked to reassure Nathan and, if I were honest, myself as I laid out the precautions I'd taken. "We have the security team working with us. The place will be locked down tighter than Fort Knox. No one gets in without an invite. We know everyone that's coming. Hell, we've even got Rod, who's a registrar, to perform the ceremony. I've covered all the bases. Nothing is going to ruin or stop this wedding, nothing." I put as much conviction into my voice as I could.

Nathan's worry didn't disappear completely, but his stiff posture relaxed a little as he leant against the bar. "Cool, it looks like you've thought of everything—"

"Hey, arsehole, you do know what I used to do for a living?"

He held up his large hand in peace offering, his eyes sparkling with amusement. "Yeah, yeah, but you never had to do it for the love of your life before."

"Point taken, but that's why I've gone over everything, triple checked it and then got Nix to go over it. I'll not take any chances with *anyone*. Those bastards won't get another chance to hurt what's precious to me."

Through the remainder of the evening, long after Nathan had disappeared up to his office, that thought lingered. I'd promised once before to keep Ferron safe, and I'd failed. It was never going to happen again. I didn't doubt my abilities, but Nathan's fears had added a niggling worry I might have missed something. Had I covered all our bases?

Nix is happy with everything, so stop stressing.

My sigh was swallowed as I finished locking the night's takings in the safe we had in the back room, then I checked the place was empty before I headed up the stairs to Nathan's apartment. I stopped on the second floor and popped my head into Nathan's office to find it empty. It was two am, so I wasn't surprised he wasn't there, but I'd no clue what time the stag party was due to finish.

Carrying on up the last flight of stairs, I paused when the door in front of me opened before I had a chance to knock. It revealed a very flushed looking Ferron. His eyes were glassy, and he wore a drunken grin. "There'ssss my Daddy. I was coming to get you," he sing-songed, a moment before his lips puckered up. "I want kisses like Lenny's getting."

He swayed as he came towards me. I barely had time to catch him as he over-balanced, giggling like it was funny that he nearly face-planted into floor. "You look like you've had a good night, little man."

I chuckled when his answer was to rest his head on my chest, snuffling much like a pig rooting for truffles. His eyes drifted closed and he mumbled, "The best." Soft little snores stroked at my ears as he went lax in my arms.

Nathan appeared in the doorway as I grappled to stop Ferron from sliding to the floor. He eyed the two of us with humour. "Lenny's not in a much better state. Do you want to stay here tonight? I'd say it will be a lot easier than trying to carry him to the car."

"You're probably right. It wouldn't do if I gave him a concussion by banging his head off a door."

Nathan stepped back as I lifted Ferron up and carried him into the apartment. Lenny lay sprawled, asleep on the sofa, and Bailey was curled up on the other end, snoring like a freight train. The room looked like a bomb had hit it. There were empty glasses, plates, clothes, and stuffed animals everywhere, and what looked like an array of bondage and sex toys scattered on the floor.

I glanced at Nathan. "What on earth have they been doing?"

He shrugged as he stared at Lenny's sleeping form. "No clue, but I can see that Lenny has brought some of our things from the playroom."

As if he'd heard his name mentioned, Lenny's eyes slitted open and peered up at us. "Sirrrr...why yous all the way over there?" he slurred as he attempted to sit up.

I swallowed my laughter when Nathan cursed. "Come on, let's get your drunken arse to bed." Before Nathan went to Lenny, he indicated down the hallway. "You know where the spare room is. Help yourself to whatever you need." With that, he lifted a swaying Lenny off his feet, much like I had done with Ferron, and disappeared a few seconds later.

Out of force of habit, I checked the door was locked before I carried Ferron in the same direction Nathan had gone, leaving the lights on for Bailey.

In the spare room, I stripped Ferron and tucked him up in bed. Not once did he open his eyes. Sensing he was going to be in a world of hurt in the morning, I went back and grabbed a bottle of juice from the kitchen and rooted through the cabinets until I found some paracetamol. Back in the bedroom, I laid them on the side then stripped off my clothing, turned the light out, and crawled in besides Ferron.

The strong scent of alcohol came off his breath as he gravitated towards me and curled into my body. I stared up at the inky darkness, listening to him breathing, my heart full of the love I felt for him. Was there room for more? Would children change things between us? They already had, I could see it, feel it. But was it for the better?

I shut my eyes as the questions continued and I struggled to find the answers.

Eight

FERRON

I didn't groan, but it was a close call when one of the girls started to cry for attention. The pounding headache I'd woken with hadn't quite abated, no matter how much fluid I'd drunk or pain pills I'd taken during the day.

The girls had both been tetchy and weren't in the best of moods. They'd both cried for their daddy, and it had broken my heart when I'd had to try and explain that Seth was at work as they'd looked at me with tear-drenched eyes.

"How do kids know just how to make you feel like utter crap? Is it like a thing that is put into their DNA when they're being created?" I asked as I got up and looked at Eddy, who looked as worn out as me.

"I've no clue, but those two definitely know how to tug on the old heart strings." As he spoke, he went to get up and I motioned for him to stay seated.

"I'll go, you went the last time." He didn't argue as he sank back down, while I walked towards the door.

Once in the bedroom, I went to Julie who was stood holding onto the side of her cot, her face full of misery. "There's a girl. You got sore gums, hey? Let's get you some medicine to see if it helps." I talked in a low voice, hoping not to wake Cheryl, who had only been down half an hour. She'd been surfing the worst, and her bottom was red raw from the vile teething nappies.

Seth had researched everything to see if there was anything that would help reduce the symptoms. The girls were both wearing amber beads around their ankles, and he'd changed up the food he was giving them, removing any citrus fruits. Now it was just a case of waiting to see if it helped.

In our bedroom, I went straight into the bathroom to get the Calpol out of the medicine cabinet Isaac had installed to keep the babies' things in. Warmth spread through me at all the little thoughtful gestures he'd made, and all the concessions he had to put up with since Seth and the girls had moved in with us. He'd not once complained, but he'd not brought up the discussion we'd had about children the other night either, and I wasn't sure why.

I'd learned not to second guess him, and that I should just come right out and ask him. I just hadn't found the right time.

You're avoiding it.

Julie took that moment to remind me I was holding her as she gave an indignant cry. "I'm sorry, is Uncle Ferron taking too long? Just give me a second and I'll get you all sorted." I talked rubbish to her as I shifted her onto my hip and worked to open the medicine bottle I'd lifted out of the cabinet.

The hold I had on her, a technique Seth had taught me to prevent me putting her down and causing her to let the whole house know how unhappy she was, allowed me to open the bottle and use the syringe to draw up the 2.5ml she was allowed. I'd quickly learned that Julie could wake the dead when she got going. It wasn't pleasant for anyone.

Once she'd swallowed the medicine, I went back into the dimly lit bedroom and sat in the old-fashioned rocking chair Isaac had found in a charity shop. The thick vee pillow was perfect to lean against and settle Julie against my chest.

The scent of Johnson's baby bath, from the wash I'd given her earlier, was all I could smell, thankfully. I cuddled her to me and started to sing a lullaby while I rocked us both. She fidgeted for a few moments as she got comfortable on my chest. Her tiny hand moved up to my cheek and she touched it in a gentle caress. My foot faltered for a moment as I attempted to swallow the feelings riding through me.

She's not yours to keep, remember. It's only for a little while till Seth finds someone to help him out.

Even as I repeated it, as I had several times over the last week and a half, it didn't help the ache that came from the thought of the girls moving back home. I sucked in a shaky breath and resumed singing in a soft voice as I made us move back and forth in the chair.

I stirred and blinked twice, looking down at my chest as I felt the warm weight pressed against me. *Fuck, I must have fallen asleep.*

Barely able to stifle the groan at the numb feeling in my arse, I inched forward a little, rocking from side to side in the hopes of getting some feeling back before I attempted to stand. Why didn't I use a cushion for the wooden seat?

Distracted, it took a second to register that there was a noise coming from the bed. My heart rattled briefly against my ribs as I shifted my gaze to look up. There, in the dim light, sat Isaac. The clothes he'd dressed in earlier to go out for his stag party were replaced with jersey pants and an old washed-out T-shirt. His hair was messy, but it was his eyes that gave me cause for concern as he sat motionless, staring at me and Julie.

When he continued to sit and stare, I offered him a timid smile. Feeling more than a little unnerved when different emotions flittered over his face, I sat forward a little more. Was he drunk?

The longer the silence stretched between us, I considered whether he'd gone into some sort of trance like drunken state. Should I say something?

"What time is it?" I whispered, to see if he was able to answer me.

"It's three o'clock," he answered immediately, sounding sober.

My brow furrowed as I tried to recall what time I'd come upstairs to sort Julie. "Have you been home long?"

His gaze met mine and something passed over his face too quickly for me to ascertain what it was, when he answered, "About an hour or so."

I tilted my head. "Why didn't you wake me?" I questioned as the strange feelings inside me increased.

His Adam's apple bobbed twice. "You looked so peaceful, so beautiful. I just wanted to look at you. Look at you both." There was something oddly intense in his expression as he shifted on the edge of the bed. The hands that had been sitting on the mattress moved to hold on to the edge. "Were you serious about wanting babies with me?"

I clutched at the little girl I held as hope bloomed wildly in my chest before I could control it. The words got stuck in my throat, so I nodded. The air got trapped in my chest as I waited for Isaac to say more.

"I want children with you," he choked out as his eyes filled with tears. "I want to see you hold our baby in your arms. I want to have a family with you."

A tear slid down my cheek as I struggled to blink them away, hearing the raw emotion in his voice. "I want that too."

His chest heaved as he got up and carefully lifted Julie's sleeping form out of my arms. He brushed a gentle kiss over my forehead. "I love you."

Recalling his words from the past to me, I grinned up at him through my blurry eyes. "Ditto, Isaac, ditto."

Nine

There were noises coming from the girls' room as Ferron lay curled up in my arms, still fast asleep. They were followed by the sound of Seth's muffled voice and one of the girls giggling. Hearing the giggles, warmth spread through my chest as I lay listening to the noises.

This last year had been a journey of discovery for both Ferron and me. Initially, I'd kept my feelings to myself and lived with the secret hope that one day he would want me. What I'd not expected was to want more than just Ferron, now that I had everything I'd wanted with him.

Seth had somehow changed that, allowing me to see what Ferron would be like as a father, what I would be like. Last Christmas had been so different to what this one was going to be. For the first time in my life, Christmas meant something more than gorging on food and watching crap TV. Not that last year hadn't been about more than that with Ferron, but we'd only been friends. This year we were engaged and about to get married.

A week today, he would become my husband and it couldn't come quick enough.

"Whatever you're thinking about, can you stop it? One of us is trying to sleep here," Ferron mumbled sleepily as he snuggled a little closer to me.

"It's Christmas, don't you want to get up and see the girls attack the presents you bought...open the presents...I bought for you?"

The moment I mentioned the girls and presents, Ferron sat up causing the duvet to fall to his waist and reveal his naked chest. Blood moved from one head to another, but before I could act, he was out of the bed.

His hands went to his hips as he stood, naked as a jaybird. "Why are you still in bed? Come on, we need to get showered and dressed." All traces of sleep were gone as he grinned excitedly at me before his naked arse disappeared into the bathroom.

Seeing the prospect of a naked, wet Ferron in my future, I jumped off the bed and went after him. The shower was already on and he stood waiting for the water to warm as I came up behind him. I wrapped my arms around him and pulled him flush against my aroused body. I slipped my cock between his thighs and he groaned as it slid under his balls.

His thighs closed tightly against my cock, right before he rocked his pelvis, giving it a sensual rub with the soft skin of his thighs.

A groan rumbled up my chest and Ferron shuddered, increasing his pace.

"In the shower, get in the shower," I demanded as I felt my orgasm build way too quickly.

"Lube, Daddy, we need lube," Ferron whined as he stepped into the shower, his body quivering with excitement.

I grabbed a bottle out of the cabinet and stepped in behind Ferron. His body, when he'd first moved in, had been rail thin, but now there were more curves to him. His bottom was plump and resembled a ripe peach. One I wanted to sink my teeth into, but foreplay was out of the question with the chance we'd be interrupted at any moment. The way Ferron was staring at me over his shoulder with impatience as I moved into the warm spray of water, I quickened my steps.

"Hurry, Daddy, I need you." As if to prove his point, he started to stroke his cock.

"You know that's Daddy's," I growled as I quickly lubed both hands. He didn't stop until my hand touched the one holding his cock. He released his grip immediately, and leant his wet back against my chest, then started to grind his arse against my fully aroused cock.

His moans and groans mixed with mine as I struggled to move away and slip my slick fingers down the crease of his arse. "Oh, little man, you're so fucking tight," I rasped out as I slid one finger into his arse after teasing the tight muscle for long seconds.

He pushed back onto my finger with a wanton moan. "More, please. I need more."

He sounded desperate and needy, making it impossible to deny him. Careful not to hurt him, I took the time to stretch him until I could easily get two then three fingers inside him. My jaw ached by the time I felt he was ready to take me.

The whining and complaining turned to cursing. Something Ferron only ever did when he was at the end of his tether. Impaling himself onto my fingers, he ground his hips back before tunnelling his cock through my loosely clasped fingers. "Fuck me, Daddy. Do it. I'm ready, I swear I am."

His voice rang off the wet tiles as I lost my control and did as he asked.

Sweat mixed with the steamy water pouring over my head as I slowly eased into Ferron. His channel convulsed around my cock, clasping it tightly. My balls started to pull up as my own arse tingled with pleasure.

"Fuck, little man!" By the time my hips were flush with his arse, I could hardly think straight. It never got old slipping into his body bare. He didn't give me much chance to catch my breath as he mewled and his arse clamped down hard enough to make me see stars.

Then he started to rock against my groin, slowly at first, but that didn't last long as he chased his orgasm. My legs started to shake as I struggled to catch my breath at his increased pace and with my knees bent to accommodate the height difference between us.

His body arched as his arms came up and his hands hooked around the back of my neck. "Harder, Daddy," he whispered in a strangled, pleasure-filled voice.

"Anything you want, my gorgeous boy." I released his cock and took hold of his hips as I bent my legs more and thrust deeper.

He grunted, then shouted, "More, Daddy."

The tight clasp and his needy demands were my own undoing. I tightened my hold and sped up. The sounds of wet flesh slapping together filled the shower stall. I wasn't sure which of us was moaning the loudest, but right then, I didn't care. All I wanted was to give the love of my life everything he wanted.

His fingers dug painfully into the flesh of my neck as he arched, shuddered, and his arse clamped around my cock. Sensations flooded my body as his cum painted the tiled wall in front of him while he shivered and juddered against me. With one final thrust, my balls pulled up and I fell over the orgasmic cliff with Ferron.

He mewled as his cock tried to release yet more cum as mine filled his arse.

I staggered back and hit the glass door as I tried to right us, while Ferron clung on to my neck to keep himself upright. My chest heaved in time with Ferron's as I shifted to rest my back against the cool tiles to regroup.

Long moments later, Ferron twisted his neck so he could look up at me. There was a lazy, satisfied smile on his face. "Merry Christmas, Isaac."

I lowered my head until my mouth was a mere inch from Ferron's. With my eyes locked on his, I opened my heart, hoping he could see the love I felt for him. "Merry Christmas, Ferron."

He moved the inch separating us and kissed me with a passion that worked to reignite my arousal.

When his mouth released mine, we were both breathless. He shifted, causing my cock to slip from his arse before he faced me. His hands reached up to cup my cheeks as he stood on his tiptoes. "Last Christmas you gave me the gift of sharing your home with no expectations of more. Little did I know how you'd change my life. I love you and I can't wait to be your husband."

His eyes were bright as I worked to swallow past the lump in my throat. "The same goes. You are it for me and have been for a long time. I love you with everything I am."

He blinked several times, but as his mouth opened, I heard the sound of distant knocking on what I thought was our bedroom door. With a sigh of disappointment, I gave his pouting lips a quick kiss. "Looks like playtime is over for us."

"Yeah, but only for now," Ferron said, while he gave me a saucy wink that a few months ago would have shocked me.

"Promises, promises."

"No, Daddy, that's a threat," he jeered before he started to giggle.

Hearing a second knock, I opened the shower door and shouted, "Give us five." Shutting the door to stop the floor getting wet, I hoped Seth had heard me.

"We'd better hurry," I muttered half-heartedly. I held my hands up to ward Ferron off as he approached with a cloth and bar of soap. "We don't have time for that."

Ferron's expression caused my heart to skip as it turned playful. "Shall we find out?"

Ten

FERRON

As the girls had no clue what Christmas was, we'd decided to sort the meal first. It was a unanimous vote to eat Christmas dinner at lunch time so the girls could go for a nap straight after and we'd all be able to relax. I'd started the prep work after I'd put the small turkey in the oven, deciding to go traditional this year with Seth and the girls, who could have it as long as it was cut up small or puréed when it came to the meat.

Isaac was busy getting the girls dressed, and thankfully leaving me alone in the kitchen. I'd been pleased when Seth had asked Isaac to help him. He couldn't cook, but that didn't stop him from trying to interfere.

My head tilted as I heard the sounds of laughter and squealing coming from the living room. A grin spread over my face as I put the potatoes into the oven to cook. The scent of roasting turkey filled the kitchen and my empty stomach growled.

The shower had delayed us from coming downstairs, and Isaac had proved his point. It had taken more than five minutes to make sure he was clean. I squirmed, recalling Seth's knowing stare when we'd entered the living room to find him playing on the floor with the girls.

Heat spread up my neck, and I blamed it on the hot cooker as I glanced down at my old, baggy joggers I'd opted to wear while cooking. Happy no one would notice where my head had gone, I diverted my attention back to the cooker, checking everything was ready. The pots were full of vegetables, ready to cook when I deemed the time was right.

Seeing there was little else for me to do, I strolled into the lounge, having gone via the fridge to grab a couple of frozen yogurt tubes for the girls to suck on.

The second I entered the room, both girls turned in unison to glance in my direction. Seth and Isaac rolled their eyes when the girls got up off the floor and toddled over to me with their arms outstretched.

"Fes," Julie cooed.

Cheryl, not wanting to be outdone, screeched, "Fet."

"Oh my god, did you hear that? They're trying to say my name." Excitedly, I got down onto my knees to cuddle both girls

"You're hearing things," Isaac muttered grumpily.

I gave him a withering stare over the top of the two dark headed girls. "You're just jealous. You heard them, didn't you, Seth?"

"Leave me out of it. They haven't attempted to say Daddy yet. I thought with you calling Isaac that all the time they might try it." He sounded as disgruntled as Isaac, but it gave me pause as I met Isaac's distressed face.

"Crap, I'm sorry, man. I didn't even think about that in front of the girls." Isaac's pinched expression left me wanting to go to him, but the girls chose that moment to cling off my neck as they attempted to climb up me like a climbing frame.

"No, sorry." Seth tugged at his uncombed hair and gave us both an apologetic smile. "That didn't come out right. I've no issue with the girls learning to understand there are different types of relationship dynamics. I mean shit, I'm a sub. Or, I was, until Rupert left—"

Unable to stand the tension pouring off him, I interrupted him. "We get it. Seriously, it's not an issue as long as it's not one for you or the girls. The last thing we'd want is to make them or you unhappy. And yeah, hearing the word Daddy might get them to say it."

Isaac got up off the floor and laid a hand on Seth's shoulder. "You only need to say if there's an issue, okay? Neither Ferron nor I will have a problem with you telling us what you want for the girls."

Seth sniffed and glanced away as if he were trying to pull himself together, which was confirmed when he looked back. His eyes were brimming with tears. "Thanks, that means a lot."

Julie squealed in delight as she pulled on my hair, causing me to yelp at the sharp tug of pain. "Hey, munchkin, you aren't supposed to pull Uncle Ferron's hair." In response, she tugged it again and gave me a toothy, drooly grin.

I tapped on her nose as Seth came to retrieve her.

"Want to open some presents? See what Father Christmas bought you?" Seth asked while he picked Julie up and cuddled her into his chest, but it was Cheryl who started to babble as she crawled off my lap to follow him. Her excitement was palpable, her tiny body appearing to quiver as she toddled towards the large Christmas tree tucked into the corner of the room.

"Wow, look at her, she knows what we're talking about." In my amazement, I didn't consider the pine needles that were constantly falling off the tree. Whereas Isaac, it seemed, had. He launched himself after the barefoot Cheryl.

"Cheryl, careful of the sticky pines," he shouted in fright, just as she let out a big wail.

Isaac scooped her up a second later and she clung to him, tears running down her face as she bellowed at the top of her lungs. Julie, not wanting to be outdone by her sister, started to wail loudly too.

A panicked look morphed onto Isaac's face as he checked Cheryl's bare foot before he started to make soothing noises.

It took several minutes of coaxing and a chocolate biscuit to get the girls to settle down enough to bring the presents out of hiding from behind the tree.

Wide eyes stared at the two little sacks I'd made with their names on. I'd had one as a child and I'd kept it. It now sat under Isaac's tree, along with the one I'd bought him last year. Only this year, they were both full of gifts we'd bought each other.

Once the girls were happily playing with the wrapping paper, and I'd taken hundreds of pictures to remember the occasion, I went back to check on the dinner.

A feeling of contentment I hadn't really felt at Christmas since my parents died, returned. Throughout the wonderful day, it reminded me why Christmas was my favourite time of year.

I'd played with and fed the girls their lunch, while laughing at Isaac's antics as he'd tried to encourage Julie to eat a sprout. There'd been much laughter and a real family feeling as the sky had started to darken as the day wore on. The girls finally went down for a nap, by which point I was exhausted, so I curled up on Isaac's lap and settled in to watch the movie he'd picked.

Seth gave a little cough. "I'll go up to my room, leave you two to it."

I glanced at him and shook my head. "Why? You don't want to watch The Old Guard? I've heard it's a great movie with the hottest gay couple. Come on, sit and relax. You know the girls will be up soon enough and have you run ragged."

Isaac's arms tightened a fraction, and I rubbed my cheek against his chest.

"If you're sure?" Seth answered with little conviction.

"We are. Sit, relax, and drink your glass of wine." Isaac didn't give Seth a chance to argue as he shifted his gaze back to the TV. He picked up the remote off the sofa cushion next to us and pressed play. Music filled the room as he dropped the remote and clasped his arm back around me.

I nestled against the warmth of his chest. The twinkling lights on the tree were the only light in the room. They cast tiny colourful reflections over every surface. The roaring fire crackled and the scent of cinnamon drifted up from the candles placed at the sides of the fireplace. A silent tear slid down my cheek as happiness welled inside me.

I closed my eyes and hoped against hope that my parents could see how happy I was. How lucky I was to find that person who wanted to give me a world full of happiness. It was truly a blessing and one I'd learned I'd fight tooth and nail to keep.

Eleven

ISAAC

It had been nigh on impossible not to think about what had happened this time last year. I'd spent an age, as had Nathan, going over security for tonight's New Year's Eve celebrations. Last year they'd been cancelled because of Devon's crazy actions. Nathan and Carl had even debated whether or not to hold a party this year, but both Ferron and Lenny had insisted it should go ahead.

I got why they wanted to have the party. That, however, didn't stop a little part of me reliving all the events that had led up to Ferron ending up in the hospital.

"If you keep scowling like that, you're going to frighten the girls before we go to work."

Ferron's voice penetrated past the worry and pulled me from my thoughts. I glanced up at him. "I'm sorry, little man...I've a lot on my mind." As I'd spoken, I'd worked on smoothing out my features.

"All that heavy thinking better be connected to the wedding and not about what happened last year. You and Nathan need to let it go. It's driving me and Lenny nuts. We both feel like we can't take a breath without either of you breathing down our necks." He stomped his foot on the carpeted floor, a flash of deep red coating his cheeks.

I got off the sofa, where I'd come to sit and...brood while I'd waited for him to get ready for work. Something else he'd insisted on, working with me when I'd wanted him to stay home, stay safe tucked up with the girls. Only he'd insisted we were going to spend the night together and I wanted that, I did, but...

I left the thought there as he came to me and took hold of my hands, a sympathetic smile appearing on his face. "I get it, I do. But any time you spend worrying about that bastard, is a minute too long. He's not worth it." He sucked in a deep breath and his hands tightened around mine. "You've made all the difference to my life. From tomorrow, you're stuck with me forever." He offered me a cheeky grin and his stiff posture relaxed when I returned it with one of mine.

"I'm stuck with you, hey?" I bent over him until my nose touched his. Joy sparkled from him. "That's just the way I want it, a forever with you, me, and a family." My voice was thick with emotion and Ferron's warm breath touched my face as he sighed.

"You really don't play fair. Let's get out of here before Nathan starts to call us to find out where we are."

I let him guide me to say goodbye to the girls and out the door to the truck. I checked the security guys were following us as we exited the drive and headed down the road towards the main street.

The traffic was light as it was still early evening. The car radio played crap eighties music that I'd never admit to knowing most of the artists from as Ferron hummed along.

When we eventually pulled into the underground parking, I double-checked no one was lurking in any dark corners. Even though I didn't sense anyone was nearby, I rang Nathan for him to confirm on the security cameras that it was safe to exit the truck. Ferron muttered under his breath words I didn't quite catch, but he waited for me to open his door before exiting the truck, once I was happy.

We went through the same process before I'd let him travel up in the lift. Devon had hidden in the stairwell last year, so I wasn't taking any chances. By the time we were in the Playroom, having gone a convoluted route we'd not normally take, Ferron was looking slightly freaked out.

His safety was of upmost importance to me. "I'm just keeping you safe," I reminded him.

He hesitated in the doorway to the bar and gave me a look I couldn't interrupt. "Just make sure you keep yourself safe as well...I'll never recover if anything happens to you. Just remember that when you're looking out for me."

There was no chance to reply as he stalked off to the bar and greeted several of the staff. I followed him slowly and thought about what he'd said. Was I putting myself at risk because I was too busy worrying about him? There was no easy answer, but I would heed his words.

Lenny came in the door behind me, quickly followed by Nathan, and I clamped my lips together to stop the laughter escaping at the frustrated expressions they wore. Only when Lenny hightailed it past me to go to the bar did I grin at Nathan.

"Why does he always have to be some damn prickly?"

"Because he's a sub and wants to test his Dom," I answered helpfully.

Nathan gave me a glacial stare that a weaker man would have cowered at. I just laughed and slapped at his back. "Welcome to my world."

His face morphed into a smile. "Would we have it any other way?"

I chuckled as I shifted my gaze to Ferron, who was talking to Lenny in an animated fashion. The love inside me only seemed more with each passing day. Would I want to change it?

I returned my gaze to Nathan and grinned. "Not on your life."

The following morning, more than a little bleary-eyed, I walked into the kitchen and had a moment of disappointment to find it empty. A scowl formed as I remembered that Ferron had decided to spend the night at Nathan's.

I rubbed at my face and sighed forlornly as I eyed the empty coffee pot that Ferron would normally have set up, ready for me to start the day. My feet dragged over the warm flooring as I stopped at the kettle to switch it on.

If I were honest, it wasn't the lack of coffee that was bothering me, it was the lack of sleep. I'd missed having Ferron curled up next to me. Add in all the worry I'd carried through the evening about Ferron's safety, and I'd not been able to settle until daybreak.

I'd had no clue that Ferron had his wedding suit delivered to Lenny or that he'd arranged with Nathan to collect everything he'd needed from the house two days prior. Ferron had been insistent on following tradition, where the groom didn't get to see his groom before the wedding. No amount of arguing that we'd already seen each other as it was one am when the club had shut the doors on New Year's Day had persuaded him otherwise.

Another sigh followed the sound of the whistle of my kettle. I didn't get two steps before Seth appeared behind me holding the twins in his arms. My mood brightened immediately as they gave me wide grins.

"There's my girls. Are you two ready to help me celebrate marrying Uncle Ferron."

"Fes, fes, fes," chanted Julie.

A frown marred Cheryl's tiny face as she glanced at Julie and said in a loud voice, "Fet."

Seth rolled his eyes and my brow wrinkled. "Whatever you do, do not tell him Julie and Cheryl argued over his name, I'll never hear the end of it."

The put-upon tone got a raised brow from Seth, but he nodded. "They never say Daddy," he griped.

As if to prove his point, Cheryl started to chant, "Fet, fet, fet."

Seth shook his head. "Come on, troublemakers, let's get you something to eat before we get you ready for the wedding."

My stomach fluttered with nervous excitement. *I was getting married!*

Twelve

I wasn't sure who was more nervous, me or Lenny. It was definitely a close call. I'd picked him to be my best man, and right now he looked anything but pleased about it. He looked a little green about the gills as he paced in front of me.

"What if I mess up the speech? I've practiced with Nathan, but he just tells me to stop worrying."

His ginger hair was styled back off his face so I could clearly see the worry in his eyes as he passed me again. His suit was teal green, and though I'd thought it would clash with his hair when he'd mentioned it, I'd been wrong. The suit was perfect. It fitted the long lines of his body and made me a little envious that he was several inches taller than me.

He'd paired the suit with a crisp white shirt and a tie in a deep pink. The buttonholes Isaac had picked were an array of colourful buttons attached to felt that had the tiniest playing card tucked into the back, so it lay flush against the lapel of the suit jacket. They were beautiful and hinted as to the theme of the wedding, of which Isaac had remained tight-lipped.

The nerves that had started to kick in the moment I'd woken without Isaac next to me, made their presence felt as Lenny continued to fret. "Will you stop pacing, you're making me nervous and we still have thirty minutes before I'm allowed to go down to the Flamingo Bar."

Lenny stopped and gave me an apologetic smile. "Do you want a glass of the champagne Nathan opened for us?"

I shook my head. "I haven't eaten, and if I drink, I'll probably make a fool of myself by saying the wrong thing at the wrong time. The fact we haven't had a run-through, and I've only had Rod trying to coach me on when I can speak, I'm already sure I'll fuck up."

Lenny's brow arched.

"What?"

"You swore. You hardly ever do that; you must be worried."

With him pointing it out, it only made the butterflies turn into a huge hornet's nest of flying vipers, determined to poke at me.

As I went to run my hands through my hair, Lenny shouted, "Don't mess your hair! It took me an age to get it just right."

I dropped my trembling hands and changed my mind about the drink. "Alcohol, give it to me. I'm never going to get through this without it." Lenny didn't hesitate, so I got up and followed him across the room to the counter to retrieve the open bottle and the two flutes sat next to it.

Three gulps in and I could already feel the effects of the sweet-tasting champagne. I didn't let the wine linger in my mouth as I finished off the first glass in record time and held the empty flute out to Lenny. "More, please."

"Shit, are you sure? If I get you pissed, Isaac will kick my arse." Even as he complained, he filled my glass again.

He eyed me warily as I immediately lifted it to my lips.

I hesitated, then sighed resignedly as I put the glass down. "Okay, okay you can stop looking at me like that. I'm getting married, I'm allowed to overreact. You wait till it's your turn."

Lenny's face became the same colour as his hair, and he lowered his gaze. The alcohol buzzing through me made it take a few seconds longer to twig what might have happened to cause the deep blush. "Did Nathan propose?" I blurted out.

His gaze remained somewhere between our shiny shoes as he mumbled, "I'm not supposed to say, so as not to spoil your day."

I reached for Lenny and gave him a happy shake, glad that I'd already put down my glass. "This is wonderful. Oh my, you're getting married to Nathan. When did he propose? Was it romantic? Did he get down on one knee—"

"Geez, give a man a chance to answer," Lenny griped when I stopped shaking him, although his eyes were brimming with happiness.

His mouth opened just as the door to the apartment opened and he muttered a curse as Nathan walked into the room. "Later," he whispered out the side of his mouth before he gave Nathan a happy smile.

Nathan's appreciative gaze swept over Lenny before he looked at me.

I'd opted for tradition and gone with a tuxedo in navy with thin silk lapels. The shirt was powder blue, and instead of a dickie bow, I'd gone for a cravat in navy silk flecked with red dots that matched my waistcoat. I'd wanted something a little fun, and I'd matched my sexy lace boy shorts and socks to the colour theme, only they were red with navy spots.

The buttonhole attached to my lapel was matched to my colour theme. The playing card was the king of hearts and I'd got misty eyed when Lenny had attached it to my suit.

"Isaac is a very lucky man, you look stunning, Ferron." The croak to Nathan's voice brought a lump to my own throat.

Lenny tucked his arm through mine. "Isaac is going to swallow his tongue when he gets a load of him, right, Sir?"

I didn't get a chance to answer when Nathan glanced at his wristwatch and then grinned. "It's show time."

Whisked down in the lift, my hands were clammy as I asked Lenny for the tenth time if he had Isaac's wedding ring.

Although Isaac had insisted he didn't need another ring, I wanted him to have one. As I already had his measurements, I'd gone ring hunting with Lenny the week before. We'd taken Nix to help guide us to something Isaac would like. I'd hit pay dirt with the engagement ring through sheer accident. His wedding ring I'd not wanted to leave to chance.

The platinum band he wore with our initials inscribed was special, but I'd wanted something else for his wedding band. I'd found it in a quaint shop that was run by an eccentric lady who made jewellery that she advised suited her mood on the given day.

Nix had been the first to see the black banded ring that turned out was onyx. The jeweller had hand cut the stone into different shapes, then placed them in an intricate pattern into a band of platinum. When the light caught the stone, it glowed with life. She'd managed to get it sized correctly to fit Isaac in the limited time I'd had, and Nix had picked it up yesterday.

Lenny's hand slipped into his trouser pocket and he pulled out the ring and laid it on the palm of his hand. "It's right here. I told you, I've got your back."

The lift doors opened, and my gaze was drawn to the large, stuffed Cheshire cat that sat at the entrance to the bar. It grinned manically at me and laughter burst out of me. Had Isaac gone all Mad Hatter on me?

I shifted my gaze back to the two men standing holding hands. "Is this what I think it is?"

"What do you think it is?" Nathan fired back, not answering my question.

"Has Isaac gone with a Mad Hatter themed wedding?" The laughter remained in my voice as I glanced back at the cat.

"Yep, and boy, wait till you see what the bar looks like," Lenny added excitedly before Nathan could stop him.

Nathan shook his head at Lenny who shrugged sheepishly before he let go of Nathan's hand and stepped to me. "Sir, you better go in and check on Isaac. We'll wait for the cue of the music."

When Lenny stood in front of the door, blocking my view, I swallowed my complaint, knowing it would be petty when I'd get to see the room in a minute.

Lenny fussed with my cravat, then looked at me with an intensity I didn't often associate with the happy-go-lucky man. "Last year, things were pretty shit. This right now, this is what happens when you spread shit on something, it helps things grow. The love between you and Isaac came from that. Don't let...anyone spoil it."

I coughed out a laugh at the analogy. "Thanks, I think."

"It's the best I got..." he trailed off as the opening bars to "The Sun is Rising" by Britt Nicole came through the door and the words struck my heart. *You're gonna make it, you're gonna make it. The night can only last so long.*

A sob caught in my throat as the doors opened and the song continued as I stepped through the doorway. *Lift up your eyes and see the sun is rising.*

I met Isaac's loving gaze.

It was time to look beyond the clouds to the future.

Thirteen

The second Ferron's bright eyes met mine, all my anxiety melted away. The stress to get to this point, to make it perfect, didn't matter when he looked at me like I'd hung the moon and the stars as he walked with confidence to where I was stood under the archway that Boyd had created.

I wasn't sure if Ferron even noticed the décor because not once did he break our connection until he came to a stop and the music faded into the final note. Hope that he'd understood why I'd picked that song stayed present as his clammy hand took hold of my equally clammy fingers and he held on tightly.

"I love you," he announced, bold and unapologetic, before anyone else could utter a word.

There were titters of laughter and some applause, but I paid it no mind as I answered him. "I love you with all that I am."

"It seems we've started in reverse. Maybe we could take a couple of steps back," Rod interjected, and the room erupted with laughter. Ferron glanced at the room, his eyes widening as if he'd just noticed we weren't alone. Or was it the décor of the room?

When he returned his gaze to mine, it was brimming with laughter and he confirmed my suspicions it was the latter. His lips twitched, but he remained silent as Rod gave a cough and started to speak.

I wasn't sure what we'd said, but I assumed I'd answered in all the right places when before I knew it, Ferron slipped a ring on my finger. "Life has a way of taking away those most precious to us. But sometimes it gives back something to balance out the loss. I wish our parents were here today to see how happy you've made me. I hope they're smiling down on us, raising a glass and offering us their blessing." Ferron licked at his lips as the ring settled at the base of my finger. "You're truly a gift, Isaac. You have given me a place to find the light of happiness at a time when all I could see was darkness. I'll love you through this lifetime and on into the next. You're my forever love, Isaac Corrigan."

My heart stuttered in my chest as I tried to quell the tears that balled in my throat. I swallowed twice as Nix stepped up and handed me the ring I'd bought for Ferron. The band had been encrusted with diamonds, emeralds, rubies, and sapphires. It sparkled under the glitter ball that twirled above our heads.

His breath appeared to catch as I slipped the ring onto his finger. "Your words were so pretty I'm not sure I can match them." There was more laughter, but I kept my gaze on Ferron. "I've loved you for many years. You were a secret dream, one I kept tucked inside my heart until I was ready to take a chance. You showed me how to be brave, how to fight for what I wanted, to share my love with you openly. You'll be my forever love, Ferron Robertson."

There were collective sighs as I didn't wait for Rod to say his final bit and declare us husband and husband. Instead, I lifted Ferron up and kissed him, kissed him with everything I felt, with every emotion that was swirling through me as I offered him everything I was.

When I finally put Ferron down, he was flushed and panting. He didn't look at the crowd behind us as Rod muttered, "You could've given me thirty seconds, man."

Ferron's expression turned sheepish as he offered a small smile to Rod.

"I pronounce you husband and husband," Rod said, loud enough to be heard over the jovial cheers.

It took a good hour before we were able to rest our hands. My wrist ached from all the hand shaking I'd done. Only then did I get to enjoy the surprise on Ferron's face as he stared at the decorated room, pointing out all the things that Boyd and his team had created.

The archway of playing cards was a thing of beauty. The large teacup and teapot were amazing, and already the twins were having the time of their lives running around them. The little matching frilly navy dresses they wore remained, much to my surprise, unstained up to now, though how long that would last was anyone's guess.

Seth had asked about the theme of the wedding, and he'd picked the shoes to match the theme. They had Alice and the rabbit on them. I loved that he'd wanted the girls to be a part of our special day. Julie toddled up to Ferron, her hands reaching up as she chanted "Fes, fes, fes."

Ferron bent and picked her up, his face bright with pleasure. "I'm your favourite uncle, hey?" he tweaked the end of her nose, making her giggle and bounce on his hip.

I gave a loud, mournful sigh before giving in and grinning at them both. "How can I blame her for loving her Uncle Fes?"

Ferron giggled just like Julie before Seth came to retrieve her.

"Come on, munchkin, it's time to eat something before you become a little miss cranky pants." Seth whisked her away in the direction of Cheryl, who was sat on a chair next to Sawyer. She was talking animatedly to him as he looked to be listening intently.

"I can't believe you managed to get all this done in eight weeks," Ferron said, drawing my attention back to him. His expression was slightly overawed as he glanced about the room once again.

"Everyone pulled together. I can't take all the credit for it. Boyd, Nathan, Sam, Scott, Nix, and so many more all helped to pull it off. The question is, was it worth it, little man?"

His breath shuddered out of him as he gave me a sappy grin. "Yes, a hundred times, yes. Look at the place, it looks amazing. Lenny's cake is a work of art." He pointed to the three-tiered hats that sat at a sloped angle, as if the hats were tumbling down. It was a marvel of engineering. The icing was bright blue, covered with playing cards that had been delicately made of icing. They were tiny, perfect replicas.

"Wait till you taste them?"

"Them?" He got a fevered light in his eyes when he stared at me.

"He made three different kinds of cake. One for each hat." I hadn't finished talking before Ferron was dragging me over to the laden table that held a Mad Hatter tea party style buffet.

It turned out that I wasn't the only one who had a sweet tooth. And I'd made sure that I'd sussed out his favourites before asking Lenny to make samples. People moved aside, seeing what I was sure was the steely determination on his face as he dragged me behind him.

At the table, Lenny appeared suddenly and slapped Ferron's hand. "No! You don't touch the cake till it's been photographed, and you've eaten some proper food."

"Cake is proper food," Ferron shot back.

Lenny shook his head, then gave a mournful sigh as he gave me a sly wink. "You sure you made the right decision marrying this heathen?"

Ferron laughed heartily. His face was alive with happiness and my heart felt like it might burst out of my chest.

"It was the only decision. Look at him."

Lenny made a gagging noise, but I didn't pay him any attention as Ferron's gaze swept over my black tuxedo and crisp white shirt before coming back to my face. "Right back at you. Look at you."

The music playing in the background silenced as the DJ spoke over the microphone. "Let's have the two grooms on the dance floor for the first dance."

The room grew eerily quiet as Ferron clutched at my hand as I led him to the middle of the floor. I'd wanted to keep some aspects of tradition and this was one of them. As I took him in my arms and nodded to the DJ, I sent up a silent prayer that Ferron would get the true meaning behind the words of the song I'd picked.

Lauren Daigle's angelic voice filled the room. The song "You Say" started as I swayed with Ferron in my arms. I held his gaze captive as I sang softly to him. *"You say I am strong when I think I am weak. You say I am yours and I believe. What you say of me I believe."*

His throat worked hard as his eyes misted over, but not one tear fell as he held my gaze. The adoration, the love, everything I'd come to recognise pulsed between us as I continued to tell him how he was so much more than he sometimes believed. Because I knew that in his heart, he believed me. Believed in the love we had, and that right there was more than I could ever have wished for.

It's the end for this pair's journey, but if you want to read where it started you can find that in Ferron's Journey: Trilogy. If you like to try something different from the author read on for a bonus chapter from The Light Beneath the Dark.

PROLOGUE

LINCOLN

Bile rose up my throat as I entered the hospital and its scent invaded my senses. I'd only ever had bad experiences when I came into this place, and the hairs on the back of my neck standing up and my gut clenching, told me this time wouldn't be any different.

As I approached the front desk, the sound of my boots hitting the floor drew the attention of the sleepy-eyed woman who manned it. Her visible jerk and widening eyes were a reaction I was used to, so I kept my face a neutral mask.

"Can I help you?" Her southern drawl was filled with anything but friendliness.

"My sis called, she's havin' a baby. I'm her birthin' buddy." I rasped, and this time my lips twitched at the horror crossing the woman's face.

Her cheeks paled as her gaze roamed over me. I was sure she'd missed nothing, from my six foot five inch height, to the black leather I wore, to my long, wavy, dark brown hair I'd not bothered to brush in my haste to get here.

The call I'd gotten an hour ago from my sister to say she'd gone into labor early, filled me with dread. I'd somehow blocked out this possibility when she'd insisted on me being there for her. I'd been there for her throughout our shitty lives, and this was no different and she knew it. Even if I didn't have the first clue as to what I was doing. I mean, I'm a thirty-five-year-old tattoo artist who runs a motorcycle club. How the fuck was I supposed to be someone's birthin' buddy for fucksake?

"Her name?" the woman squeaked.

"Lizzie Stone."

The sounds of tapping filled the dead air between us and I scraped my booted foot on the floor as I glanced about, only seeing one other guy, slouched sleeping on one of the plastic chairs. A Tuesday in the hospital seemed to be a slow night. I'd have to remember that the next time I needed to come.

I hated sitting waiting for hours for some trainee to come and patch up whatever injury I'd gotten from fighting. They always gave me someone that looked like their Mamma still had to wipe their ass.

"It appears your sister is booked into the maternity ward, it's on the second floor." She pointed behind me. "Take the elevator to the second floor, turn right as you exit, and go straight down to the double doors. There's a bell to press to call for attention. They'll check with your sister before you can enter," she warned, and I rolled my eyes.

I glanced at the bank of elevators before giving her a nod. "Thanks."

In the elevator I rubbed at my eyes, trying to get rid of the tired feeling. I'd been up till one in the morning, finishing a tattoo on a prospect to the club. Quinn, aka Rattlesnake, had given me a headache as he'd whined and fucking moaned about how painful it was. Was it my fucking fault he'd chosen to have a rattlesnake tattooed from one hip bone to the other? I'd warned the stupid fuck it would be painful over bone, but he'd insisted.

I'd had a few moments of doubt, wondering whether we'd made a mistake giving him entry into the club the way he bitched, but he'd not passed out or asked me to stop, so that was something. Sid, my second in command and otherwise known as Serpent, had passed out cold the first time I'd tattooed him. He'd never lived it down, and the old crew still gave him shit for it.

The elevator chimed as it reached the second floor and, walking out of the elevator, I rolled my shoulders to ease the stiffness in my upper back from being hunched over. Turning right, I headed down the hall that smelled of disinfectant, though the scent didn't quite mask the odor of blood and guts.

The couple of people roaming the hallway dressed in dark green scrubs gave me a wide berth as my feet thudded loudly in the nearly empty hallway. The walls were painted a pale rose color and held some cheery pictures.

Reaching the door, I pressed the bell and waited, looking into the security camera.

"Hello, how can I help?" asked a tiny female voice.

"My sister rang me, Lizzie Stone. She's in havin' a baby. I'm Linc Stone, you should be expecting me. I'm her buddy to help her through this," I muttered, heat riding up my face at the silence that followed. I'd bet my last dollar the woman was probably comparing me to my tiny sister, with her angelic face. People often questioned our relationship until they looked at our eyes. The deep brown was threaded with gold and, depending on mood, could look more gold than brown.

It was the only good thing we'd gotten off our Pop. Mercifully, the mean ass fucker was long gone, so wouldn't get anywhere near this new baby to spread his hate.

"I'll need to check before I can let you in."

The tiny voice pulled me from a place I didn't really want to go and I watched the light above the camera go out. I stood like a dick, kicking at the floor. Why had I agreed to this?

The issue was, I'd do anything for my baby sister and she knew it. She had conned me when her fly-by-night ex had done a runner. What I should have done was chase his deadbeat ass down and hung him up by his balls until he agreed to support her. What did I do instead? Said yes to this madness.

That's why I'm here in the middle of the night, getting ready to tell her to breathe, and avoid looking at her pushing a tiny human out of her body!

What the fuck was I thinking?

Blaming the warmth in the hall for the sweat gathering around my hairline, I took off my leather jacket, leaving me in just the short-sleeved T-shirt I'd dragged on after the call. I glanced down and didn't get a chance to swear when there was a buzzing sound and the door was released. With a sweaty palm I opened the door, dragging in a deep breath to try and slow down my thundering heart.

The Killer T-shirt I wore was forgotten about as I walked down another long hall, this one in a deeper pink, past several open doors. Some rooms were empty, while others housed heavily pregnant women and what I assumed were their folks to help.

I pushed aside the fact I probably looked as terrified as some of the faces I'd seen. By the time I got to the desk, the one member of staff I'd seen initially as I'd started the long walk had morphed into five. I got the feeling whoever had answered the intercom had called their buddies to come and get a good look at me.

Belton, Texas has a relatively small population, around twenty-three thousand, and our motorcycle club is well known, if not for all the right reasons. It didn't stop the folks from coming to use the auto shop I owned to get their vehicles fixed, or to the tattoo shop I had to get inked. We paid our taxes and, on the whole, kept our noses clean...sort of. None of that made a difference to some of the folks though, who thought all bikers were just bad news.

I swallowed a sigh and tried to keep from scowling. "Lizzie Stone, where is she?" There was the sound of a loud mewl, followed by several cuss words I'd have been proud of, as a door opened behind the desk. Holy fuck, what were they doing to the woman?

Icy dread ran through me as I recalled Lizzie's insistence that I watch a few of the birthing videos on YouTube. The 'hell no' I'd stuck to might not have been the best idea.

What was I walking into? Right then, I'd have preferred running into a rival motorcycle club on my own, rather than facing what was about to happen.

"If you'll follow me, I'll take you to the birthing room. Lizzie has just been taken in. I'm Anne-Marie and I'll be the midwife assisting with the birth—"

"How the fuck can you be assisting if you're standin' here," I ground out harshly.

She took a step back, her face flushing rosily. "Erm...well...I was waiting for you," she stuttered, sounding flustered.

"Then you better get movin'." For some reason I couldn't explain, a sense of urgency took hold of me. I never gave the other women a thought as I met Anne-Marie's unprofessional glare.

"What're we waitin' for?" I raised the hand not holding my jacket and indicated she should get moving.

She swung around and huffed loud enough for me to hear, but I didn't give two fucks. The sense of unease I'd had from the moment I'd answered my phone was increasing by the second. I wasn't sure if it was just the reality of what was about to happen, or something else, but I'd always listened to my gut and it was saying 'get movin'.'

Anne-Marie led us back down the hall to a double door that required a security swipe to enter. The scent that hit my nose as we walked through was like nothing I'd smelled before, and I started to breathe through my mouth, not wanting to think about what it was.

We came to yet another desk, a woman in navy blue scrubs sitting at the computer. She looked up and I gave her ten out of ten for showing no reaction as her gaze swept over me, before going to Anne-Marie.

"Anne-Marie, I thought you were bringing Lizzie in?" Her tone was sharp and her eyes held a hint of steel.

"I was waiting for her brother. Stop fussing, Barb, I'm here now."

Something passed between the two women I didn't understand, but it felt off. I shook it off as Anne-Marie went to the door on her left and opened it. The cry of agony coming from my sister left me in a cold sweat and I was running through the door ready for battle. I stopped cold at the sight before me.

Anne-Marie chuckled and tapped my shaking arm as she passed by me, letting the door close behind her. "It's perfectly normal for Lizzie to be making these noises."

I didn't hear a word she said as I took in Lizzie. Her Stimpy pj top stopped at her bloated waist, revealing her bare ass. The back of the gurney she was on had been raised so she could hang on to it as she knelt. There were several sheets beneath her naked bottom half, covered in blood, and god knew what else, as it ran down her legs while she rocked, mewled, and cried out in distress. She seemed to repeat the pattern of rock, mewl, and cry.

The urge to run the other way was forced away by the need to make it all better, to stop what was hurting her. I felt utterly useless because this was a foe I couldn't fight. I threw my jacket onto a small two seater sofa in pale blue that was off to the side, taking a steading breath as I walked to Lizzie.

"Lizzie? Lizzie, I'm here baby girl, I got you." I avoided looking down at her lower body as I stroked her back as she'd taught me to do. Firm but not too firm. Her words ran through my head as she twisted to look at me.

Her eyes were full of tears and had black circles around them. Her skin was sweaty, and her long dark brown hair was stuck to her forehead.

"Oh thank god you're here. Help me Linc. Make the pain stop. Something's wrong, I can feel it," she cried, ripping at my heart with her anguish.

Her body rippled under my hand as I continued to stroke her. I glared at Anne-Marie, who was talking to the other woman wearing a set of pale lilac scrubs, paying Lizzie no attention. "Do something, she says somethin' ain't right."

"Now everything is fine. This is just part of birthing. The mom can get a little upset."

She got no further when Lizzie cried out, "I wanna pushhhhhh."

Anne-Marie came over and tutted. "You've only been laboring for a couple of hours. This is your first birth and it can take several hours before you'll feel the need to push."

Her tone sounded condescending to me, but as I was clueless, I bit my tongue.

But Lizzie was having none of it. "I'm tellin' you I need to fuckin' push," she panted, and took hold of my other hand, holding it in a death grip. "Make them do something," she pleaded with me after she got her breath back from another contraction.

Her whole body seemed to be alive the way it rippled and contracted. My knees weakened when I looked down between her legs and saw a pool of congealing blood. Back to breathing through my mouth, I glanced back at Anne-Marie, who didn't seem at all concerned.

Then all hell broke loose as Lizzie screamed so loudly I thought she'd burst my ear drums and the two women ran to the bed. Anne-Marie finally examined Lizzie and when she stood, her face showed real fear.

"What's wrong?"

She didn't answer as she hit the emergency buzzer at the back of the bed and people started to appear like ants coming out of the woodwork. They were everywhere. Lizzie held onto my hand, her eyes pleading with me to help.

"Can someone tell me what the fuck is going on?!" I roared to the room, my fear fully in charge.

The woman who'd been sitting outside at the desk stated, "We have no time to waste, the baby is stuck. The shoulders are wedged in your sister's pelvis, we need to get the baby out..." she trailed off as a man entered the room and she started to relay information to him, ignoring me completely.

I lowered my head to Lizzie's, my hair curtaining her face to keep her from seeing the chaos in the room. "I'm here, I'm gonna keep you safe, I swear." Even as I said it, I could see resignation fill her face with a knowledge I couldn't even fathom.

"Keep River safe. Promise me no matter what, you'll keep my baby safe. I've signed all the legal guardian paperwork and registered it with the court, so you won't have any issues." Her voice faded as her color drained. Her body went rigid and another scream froze my insides. This was followed by the cries of a baby.

"Come on Lizzie, you've got a baby to care for, stop this shit," I rasped through the ball of emotions clogging my throat. Her eyelashes fluttered and her hand went slack in mine.

About the author

Hi all,

My name is Jayne and I live in the Isle of Man. A tiny place in the Irish sea. It's an island steeped in folklore and history and just begs to have stories written about it, and one of my first inspirations. Over the last few years that has changed and now I find inspiration everywhere.

I'm an eclectic kinda girl so I've written contemporary and historical gay romance. I started with paranormal and I hope to go back to that in 2021, I'm also branching out in to crime, so let's see where that takes me. My head is so full of ideas, it could lead anywhere.

I hope you have enjoyed this book, and if you are in need of more, then you can find all my other books, on Amazon and in KU.

If you would like to give me any feedback or just have any questions, go ahead and friend me on Facebook, and I would be happy to answer anything. Well, almost anything. I hope you enjoyed this book as it was a little different for me. If you would also like to leave a review, then I would love to read your thoughts.

Thank you for taking the time to be part of my dream.

www.ingramcontent.com/pod-product-compliance
Lightning Source LLC
Chambersburg PA
CBHW030637130626
46552CB00002B/894